"I don't believe it!" Kay whirled around, and looked at her friend. "Leah Stephenson, sometimes you really *do* have all the luck!" Kay's voice was a mixture of shock, pride and envy.

Finola unpinned the notice and handed it to Leah with a flourish.

Leah quickly skimmed the piece of paper. She leaned back against the side of the stairs and attempted to read it again, this time more slowly. "I—I don't understand," she murmured, and looked from Finola to Kay and then to the dozen or so girls watching for her reaction.

"Here, love, let me read it for you." Finola brushed her mane of black hair off her face and read:

"Bay Area Ballet Company Rehearsal: 3:30 P.M., North Studio, Academy Building. First Cast, *Dance Indigo:* Stephenson, Phillips, Hogan."

"And your name, Leah, is circled with a purple Magic Marker!" Katrina tapped the paper with her finger. "Everyone knows purple is your favorite color, so you must be the Stephenson in question."

"Doesn't take a brain to figure that one out!" Pamela Hunter's voice dripped venom. "Once a teacher's pet, always a teacher's pet!"

The SATIN SLIPPERS Series
by Elizabeth Bernard
Published by Fawcett Girls Only Books:

Other titles in the Girls Only series
available upon request

RISING STAR
Satin Slippers #10

Elizabeth Bernard

FAWCETT GIRLS ONLY • NEW YORK

RLI: <u>VL 7 & up</u>
     IL 8 & up

A Fawcett Girls Only Book
Published by Ballantine Books
Copyright © 1989 by Cloverdale Press, Inc.

Library of Congress Catalog Card Number: 88-92918

ISBN 0-449-14546-8

Printed in Canada

First Edition: May 1989

With special thanks to Baryshnikov Bodywear, Bonnie August,
Body by Gilda Marx, Capezio by Ballet Makers, and Freed of
London.

To Elizabeth Rose, who always was the real dancer

Chapter 1

"So, have you heard from Alex at all?" Kay Larkin asked Leah Stephenson one cold February night as they left the San Francisco Ballet Academy. Kay wrapped her pink mohair scarf tightly around her head, then slipped her arm through Leah's. She held Leah back a little from the small group of girls heading down the dimly lit street to Mrs. Hanson's boardinghouse, where she and several other SFBA students lived.

An icy gust of wind blew up from the Bay and whipped Leah's long blond hair across her face. For a moment she held her mittened hands tight over her ears, as if trying to protect them from the cold. She was really trying to pretend she hadn't heard Kay's question.

Alex! All day long talk had been about Alexandra Sorokin, Leah's best friend—or *former* best friend. Leah didn't know which these days, now that Alex had left the school. She didn't want to hear about Alex anymore, because she missed her so much. Everything that reminded Leah of Alex hurt.

"Well, have you heard from her?" Kay insisted on knowing. "Did she call?"

Leah prefaced her answer with a sigh. "Not a word. You'd think Alex really had been kidnapped this time!" she joked. Only a couple of months ago, Leah and Kay had thought Alex had been kidnapped and taken back to her native Russia by the KGB. She had turned up, rosy and happy, and oblivious to the worry she had caused, after a Winter Festival weekend at her boyfriend's college.

At the memory of their escapade, Kay laughed. The sound made Linda Howe turn around. The tall black girl dropped back to walk with them.

"Alex is a real stinker!" she said. "I didn't think abandoning her dance career to go to college meant abandoning her friends." She shifted her dance bag from her right shoulder to her left, then added, "What really gets me is how much I miss her!"

"Miss who?" Pamela Hunter's drawl floated back on the wind. Kay and Leah groaned in unison.

Pam had been leading the parade back to Mrs. Hanson's with her sidekick Abigail Handhardt. She'd been walking at record speed, eager to be the first back for the night's scheduled lottery drawing to see who'd inherit Alex's old room. Now she waited for Leah and the others to catch up.

"They're talking about Alex, Pam," Abby whined. "Everyone misses Alex. I do, too."

Pam shrugged, then resumed walking, next to Leah now. "I don't. And at least I'm honest about it. With Alex out of the picture, the best room in the boardinghouse is up for grabs." Leah could practically hear Pam licking her lips at the prospect of moving into Alex's old digs. "And I think some of us are much better off in general without Sorokin around!"

"Speak for yourself, Hunter!" Linda said curtly, and purposely lengthened her stride to put some distance between herself and Pam.

"Well, *Leah's* better off." Pam's green eyes glinted under the streetlight.

Leah sighed, exasperated. "That's getting old, Pam. Inheriting Alex's place at the front of the barre in class was no big coup, believe me!" Leah was getting tired of Pam needling her. Ever since Alex had left the school, Leah had been forced into the spotlight—at least in Madame Preston's classes. Leah, as the one remaining Golden Gate Scholarship winner at the Academy, really felt as if she were on the spot. Though she was just fifteen and only a first-year student, she was suddenly being treated like the best dancer in the school. Part of Leah was proud of her new position; part of her quaked at the thought that she was Alex's heir apparent.

At the moment Leah wished Pam could trade places with her, at least for one day. Let Pam Hunter experience firsthand what leading the class felt like. After a day or two of dancing right under Madame's eagle eye, Leah was pretty sure that Pam would change her tune. It was no picnic, being at the front of the class.

"Finola Darling's made the most of Alex's leaving, too," Pam said scornfully. "To think she isn't even a real SFBA student and she's going to be in charge of Madame Preston's birthday gala!" Pam shook her head. "Why, I'd even prefer it if Alex had that job. Though why anyone should get so excited about putting together a dopey ballet program to honor Madame is beyond me!"

"What's wrong with Finola?" Kay asked, leaping to the defense of the exchange student from England's Royal Ballet School.

"She's not Pam!" Linda said sourly. "That's the problem."

"I wouldn't want to be in charge of any dumb gala," Pam loudly protested. "It just doesn't seem right that none of the regular students here get a chance to run things." She flipped her thick red braid over her shoulder, adjusted her furry black earmuffs, and quickened her pace. "But I, for one, don't have time tonight to dawdle on the way home. Come on, Abigail!" Pam commanded her one and only real friend. "I don't want to be late for the lottery!" Her high-heeled boots made a clicking noise as she raced down the pavement into the shadows.

"As if getting to the boardinghouse first will help her win!" Kay sounded disgusted. "I think our Pamela underestimates Mrs. Hanson."

"I must say I have mixed feelings about Alex's room myself," Linda said, and flashed a smile at Kay. Linda and Kay roomed together in the one double in the boardinghouse and both girls loved the arrangement. But Mrs. Hanson had said that she'd be willing to forgo the extra rent for the rest of the semester so that each girl could have a "place of her own." Even if Linda didn't win Alex's prize corner room, she'd move into the room of whoever did.

"I understand *why* Mrs. Hanson didn't just as-

sign the room and decided to have a lottery...."
Linda's voice trailed off and she gestured with
her head toward Pam.

Pam and Abigail were laughing their way down
the street. "Of course I'll get rid of those simply
awful curtains, and my mother promised me the
sweetest Laura Ashley spread you could possibly
imagine." Hearing Pam's plans to redecorate Alex's
space made the other girls cringe.

"Laura Ashley?" Linda mouthed, and sank in a
mock faint against a lamppost. "Spare me!"

Kay shook her head. "She'd actually kill for that
room."

"I hope she doesn't get it. Alex would hate the
idea of Pam touching anything that had once
been hers!" Linda declared in a passionate whisper. "Or covering every surface in sight with one-
hundred-percent-cotton meadows of perfectly ridiculous little flowers!"

Leah didn't want the room at all, but all her
pleading with Mrs. Hanson hadn't worked. "When
there's a lottery, every girl has to take part," Mrs.
Hanson had told her. "You'd like Alex's old room,
once you fixed it up so that you'd feel at home.
It's so much more spacious than yours, and you
won't have to climb up to the top floor when
you're tired. Anyway," Mrs. Hanson had added
with a hug, "I think Alex would have wanted you
to have it." She knew that the kindly boardinghouse proprietor was right, but since that conversation Leah had prayed with all her heart that she
wouldn't win.

The girls trooped up the front steps to the
town house and Pam threw open the door. "We're

home!" she announced. "And tonight's the big
night and—hey, what's this stuff?" Pam demanded
as she walked into the front hall. Leah and the
other girls crowded through the door behind her
to see what was wrong.

"Stuffed animals?" Linda queried.

"Some kind of toy drive?" Kay suggested.

Leah spotted a large suitcase with a dozen
airline luggage tags on it peeking out from under-
neath the heap of toys.

Abby looked uncertainly from Pam to Leah and
then shrugged. "I didn't think new students came
until next month," she commented. "Now they're
admitting them without auditions." She poked a
plush green brontosaurus and smiled. "I didn't
think anyone collected stuff like this anymore."

"A teddy bear with a tutu!" Leah said, grinning.
"Someone new must be moving in!"

"Well, whoever she is, she still has to take part
in the lottery!" Pam bristled.

Mrs. Hanson bustled into the hall, still wearing
her apron. "You're all so late, girls. Rehearsals
again?"

Pam unzipped her leather jacket and planted
her hands on her hips. "Late or not, Mrs. Hanson,
I want to know what's going on here. You promised a lottery, and obviously someone has moved
in. I hope she doesn't think she's getting Alex's
room, because if—"

"Pamela!" Mrs. Hanson broke in in a stern voice
worthy of her sister, Madame Preston. "We will
discuss this over supper. But the assignment of
rooms in this boardinghouse is not up to you.

Now come to the table, everyone, and meet our new tenant."

Leah questioned Kay with a look. After all, as SFBA's one-girl grapevine, Kay was supposed to know everything. But she shook her head and shrugged. "Beats me!" she whispered, then pushed ahead of Pam to be the first to get a glimpse of their new housemate.

Leah gawked at the sight that met her eyes. There was no young woman at the table, but a child. She peered over a tall glass of milk and looked too frightened to smile. Leah judged her to be perhaps eleven or twelve, but her figure hadn't yet developed at all. Her face was small and narrow, and she was the plainest person Leah had ever seen—except for her eyes. They were a deep, interesting hazel and seemed to fill half her face. Her pretty brown hair, which hung in two thick braids, seemed to be too long compared to the rest of her.

Suzanne Winter, who currently had the other single room on the second floor, was already at the table. She was nursing a slight knee injury and had had to beg off dancing at the gala, though she'd already volunteered to help with costumes or sets in any way she could. Now she was sitting next to the little girl. Behind her oversized glasses, Suzanne's eyes were wide. Whatever she had learned about the girl—and the lottery—had been some kind of shocker.

"Girls, this is Sophie...." Leah wasn't sure if she imagined it, but Mrs. Hanson seemed to hesitate before revealing the girl's last name. "Potter."

"Sophie Potter!" Kay screeched, and bounded

across the room. She took the startled girl's hand and pumped it hard. "You're the dancer who won that big Moscow competition! You've studied at the Vaganova Institute in Leningrad, just like Alex." Before Sophie could reply, Kay turned around. "Sophie's a prodigy!" she announced to the other girls.

For Sophie's sake, Leah cringed. But at the moment she couldn't think of a thing to say to make Sophie feel more at ease.

Kay turned her attention back to Sophie. "I'm Kay, Katherine Larkin, that is. I am right about you, aren't I?"

Sophie's voice was surprisingly deep and full. "Yes," she said, modestly lowering her eyes a little. "I won that competition and I did study at the institute last year."

Mrs. Hanson broke in and motioned for the other girls to sit down at the table. "Dinner's getting cold," she advised them, then proceeded to make the rest of the introductions. Once the soup was served, she explained that Sophie had been admitted to the school to study with Madame Preston for the next two years.

"But you're not even in high school yet!" Pam pointed out sourly.

"No," Sophie replied, and shrank back under Pam's gaze. The tall dining-room chair seemed to swallow her up.

"Sophie will take a full schedule of dance classes with the rest of you—and she will arrange her academic program around it. She'll be attending the intermediate school down the block from the Academy." Mrs. Hanson paused to give Sophie's shoulder a motherly pat, then headed for the kitchen to bring in the next course.

"I guess I don't get to start dancing until after next week," Sophie volunteered. Her small face brightened with a wistful smile. "I can't wait to work with Madame Preston!"

"*I* can't wait to hear what happened to our lottery!" Pam leaned back in her chair and folded her arms across her chest. She fingered the tiny jade heart that dangled from a chain around her neck and stared at Sophie.

As if on cue, Mrs. Hanson appeared with a platter of bread, cheese, and cold cuts in one hand and a large bowl of salad in the other. She put them down on the table and took her seat at one end. "Help yourselves. Now, about Alexandra's room ..."

Pam sat up straight and gave Mrs. Hanson her harshest glare.

Mrs. Hanson didn't flinch.

"Madame Preston has decided that Sophie will have the room," she explained firmly.

Leah breathed a sigh of relief. Across the table from each other, Kay and Linda cheered and pumped each other's hand. They would still be roommates.

"And why is that, may I ask?" Pam drummed her fingernails against the top of the table.

"She didn't tell me, Pam. I don't think she knew about our idea of a lottery."

"Then she had no right to interfere—" Pam argued.

"When it comes to the San Francisco Ballet Academy, Pamela, Alicia Preston has *every* right to interfere. This boardinghouse is run exclusively for SFBA students." Mrs. Hanson returned Pam's angry stare until the redhead looked away.

Suddenly Pam pushed her chair away from the table and jumped to her feet. "Nothing's fair around here! First they admit some—some"—She looked at Sophie—"some little girl to the school *without* an audition. Then she takes away my room!"

"I don't mind living in another room, Mrs. Hanson," Sophie said meekly, her eyes wide and frightened. But before Mrs. Hanson could speak her piece, Sophie looked directly down the table and seemed to see Leah for the first time. "Wow!" Sophie exclaimed. "You're the girl in the *FootNotes* article. I didn't connect your face with the name. Leah—Leah Stephenson. Gee, I never thought I'd live in the same boardinghouse with you!"

"I think I'm going to be sick!" Pam clutched at her stomach dramatically and stomped into the parlor, then through the door to the converted sun porch that served as her room.

"I'd better see if she's all right." Abigail got up and hurried after her friend. A moment later Pam's door closed with a resounding bang.

"Sophie, don't worry. You are going to be okay around here," Linda said enthusiastically. "I think the rest of us are perfectly happy that you ended up with Alex's room."

"Who's Alex?" Sophie asked, and within moments Leah, Kay, and Linda all began talking at once, trying to fill Sophie in on what had been happening at the boardinghouse since the start of the year.

*   *   *

An hour later the girls were still at the table enjoying Mrs. Hanson's homemade cookies and tall glasses of milk, when Sophie's mother walked in. Raul Zamora, the SFBA fencing teacher who helped out around the school, followed close behind, carrying one of Sophie's trunks. "I've come to help you unpack, Soaps!" Mrs. Potter said. Kay giggled at the nickname.

Raul carried two trunks upstairs, then left as Sophie followed her mother up the steps with an armful of dolls and teddy bears. Soon after, Leah, Kay, and Linda got up to clear the table.

"What do you think of her?" Linda asked, after checking the stairs to be sure that the Potters were out of earshot.

Leah carefully stacked the dishes in the sink and reached for the large bottle of dishwashing liquid. While she waited for the basin to fill with water, she turned to Linda. "I think I like her. She's a funny little person, but there's something interesting about her."

"She's got soul!" Kay declared, pushing Leah away from the sink and rolling up her sleeves. "I can tell. I saw a clip of her dancing on the TV news one time. It was just something simple, but she made it look—I don't know—like Pavlova."

"Pavlova?" Leah couldn't quite believe that.

"Well, you know..." Kay faltered. "She was very, very good. And she didn't look like a little girl when she was dancing."

Linda, who was waiting by the dishrack with a towel, tapped her fingers against her chin thoughtfully. "I don't know. Prodigies—that doesn't seem like Madame Preston's style to me, taking in a twelve-year-old. Why, Leah, she didn't even want you to make that ballet movie, and you're fifteen already."

Leah looked down at her feet and frowned. "Madame said I was too young as a dancer for a film career." *Temptations,* a full-length ballet feature, was now being filmed at the school. With all the commotion about Alex during the past few weeks, Leah had almost forgotten about the movie—almost, but not quite. Turning down the part had been her own decision, one she didn't regret. Still, if a twelve-year-old could be a full-time dance student at SFBA, in violation of all of the school rules, then why couldn't Leah Stephenson have been a real star at fifteen? For the first time since she'd come to the Academy, Leah thought that Madame Preston wasn't quite playing fair.

Before she could think about it further, Mrs. Hanson called Leah out of the kitchen.

Carrying a tray with a teapot and two cups on it, she guided Leah to the back wing of the house and her own small suite of rooms. Mrs. Hanson sat down, then patted the seat beside her on the overstuffed chintz-covered sofa.

"Sit down for a minute, Leah. I want to talk to you about Sophie. I know she is young for you— for all you girls really. She is talented, but she's just a little girl." Mrs. Hanson offered Leah some tea, but Leah shook her head.

After taking a sip, Mrs. Hanson went on. "Madame asked me to ask you in particular to look after Sophie. As you can see, she already looks up to you somewhat."

"But she's supposed to be such a great dancer," Leah said, then bit her tongue. She had sounded almost as snide as Pam.

Mrs. Hanson chuckled. "Yes, well, we'll all have to get used to that fact of life, now, won't we?"

Leah couldn't help but return Mrs. Hanson's kind smile. "It's hard. I mean with Alex gone and everything."

"Yes, I know you miss her. But Sophie is still a child, Leah. And when Madame interviewed her, she mentioned reading about you. She looks up to you, and I think she could use a big sister to show her the ropes. Please be the old hand at SFBA for Sophie. I told Madame we could count on you ... to fill Alex's shoes."

Chapter 2

"To fill Alex's shoes . . ." The phrase haunted Leah all night and was still ringing in her head the next morning on her way to school. Alex had not only been one of SFBA's most gifted dancers but also such a help to so many students and always a loyal, no-nonsense sort of friend. Competing with Alex for roles had been something Leah could handle. Matching up to the older, sophisticated, oh-so-wise Alexandra Sorokin as a person seemed a tall order for fifteen-year-old Leah to fill.

As she followed Kay up the path leading to the Victorian mansion that housed the school, Leah dragged her feet a little. She suddenly felt as nervous as she had last fall when she'd walked into Madame's class for the first time. Madame's faith in Leah was scary, and she wasn't sure she could measure up to the task. Leah wasn't Alex; she couldn't be. But somehow that was what Madame wanted.

"I wonder what's up?" Kay called back to Leah over her shoulder. The short, curly-haired girl

waited for Leah to join her on the trellised porch.
The front door was open, and half of the girls in
Madame's class were milling around the spacious
entrance hall.

"Is that Leah?" Katrina Gray cried, and pushed
through the crowd toward the door. "Is she here?"
Her soft voice trembled with excitement. "Oh,
Leah, wait until you hear!"

"What's up, Katrina? Did something happen?"
Leah asked, confused by all of the faces suddenly
turned in her direction.

"That's putting it mildly!" Mia Picchi grumbled
over the general din.

"You mean you don't *know*?" Suzanne pushed
her glasses up on her nose and stared at Leah in
disbelief.

"Know what?" Kay spoke up. She stood on her
toes to see exactly what everyone was looking at
on the huge floor-to-ceiling bulletin board. The
cork surface was papered with notices, but the
crowd's interest was focused on one tiny index
card pinned on the lower right-hand corner.

"Oh, Leah," Finola Darling cried with her crisp
British accent. "Come over here quick! It's jolly
good news, love!" she promised, her gray eyes
sparkling.

Leah felt herself being pushed forward toward
Finola. Helplessly, she looked at Kay, who, thanks
to a part-time job in the Academy office, was the
school's most reliable source of inside information. "Don't tell me you missed some hot gossip,
Kay," she teased, trying to make light of her feelings. Her heart was beating double-time, and she

was glad when Katrina came up to her and squeezed her hand.

"I guess I'm slipping!" Kay said cheerfully. She made her way to the board ahead of Leah and stooped down to read the notice. "I don't believe it!" She straightened, whirled around, and looked at her friend. "Leah Stephenson, sometimes you really *do* have all the luck!" Kay's voice was a mixture of shock, pride, and envy.

Finola unpinned the notice and handed it to Leah with a flourish. "C'mon, mates, keep it down to a dull roar!" she ordered. "Let her read it."

Conversation dropped to a low buzz, and Leah quickly skimmed the piece of paper. She leaned back against the side of the stairs and attempted to read it again, this time more slowly. "I—I don't understand," she murmured, and looked from Finola to Kay and then to the dozen or so girls watching for her reaction. Leah suddenly felt self-conscious. She was almost grateful when Finola took the notice from her hand.

"Here, love, let me read it for you." Finola brushed her mane of black hair back off her face and read:

"Bay Area Ballet Company Rehearsal: 3:30 P.M., North Studio, Academy Building. First Cast, *Dance Indigo:* Stephenson, Phillips, Hogan."

"And your name, Leah, is circled with a purple Magic Marker!" Katrina tapped the paper with her finger. Her soft brown eyes twinkled. "Everyone knows purple is your favorite color, so you must be the Stephenson in question."

"Doesn't take a brain to figure that one out!" Pamela's drawl dripped venom. "Once a teacher's pet, always a teacher's pet."

"Cut it out, Pam!" Finola commanded. The tall gray-eyed girl turned to Leah and offered her her hand. "I think this couldn't have happened to a better person." If Finola was disappointed, she didn't show it.

But Leah was still trying to digest the facts. In record time, her whole world had done an about-face. One minute she had been worried about measuring up to the same standards Madame had set for Alex; now she was getting the kind of lucky break that could change a dancer's life.

"It means I get to dance with the company!" Leah said, still stunned. "I—I can't believe it!" For the first time in two weeks a real smile twitched at the corners of her lips. She closed her eyes and pressed her hands to her temples. Cautiously, she opened her eyes again, then looked around. Finola, Kay, Katrina, Pam—and everyone else—were all still there, and everyone but Pam was smiling at her. Leah knew then that it wasn't a dream. If she had been dreaming, Alex would have been there, too, probably scowling at Leah's latest stroke of luck while at the same time wishing her the best.

Ever since coming to the prestigious ballet school in September, Leah had danced her heart out, determined to become a top-ranked ballerina. Lately Leah had worked doubly—no, triply hard. She had never felt so driven in her life. Suddenly it was more important than ever to prove that she, Leah Kimberly Stephenson, wasn't a quitter.

Sticking to her plan to become a professional dancer seemed even more important to Leah, after Alex's decision to give up dancing a couple of weeks ago. Even the recent breakup with her boyfriend, Peter, because seeing him interfered with her SFBA schedule, seemed worth it now.

"A professional dancer," she murmured, and suddenly the enormity of it struck her. She had been chosen to perform with the company in a revival of Madame Preston's one-act ballet, which was to premiere in two weeks on the stage of the War Memorial Opera House. Leah had always thought breaks like that happened only to movie heroines or characters from TV soap operas. But this was no soap opera: this was the tough, competitive world of SFBA. And her hard work had paid off, as somehow deep down inside she always knew it would. Silently she thanked Madame for giving her the chance to prove to the world that all of the sacrifices *were* worth it.

"One ballet does not a pro make!" Pam quipped tightly. She flipped her thick red braid over her shoulder, then turned her back and marched noisily up the sweeping front staircase toward the studios on the second floor. "You'd better not count your chickens before they're hatched, Leah!" she tossed off with a sneer from the top step. "Being late for morning class is not very professional at all!"

For a moment the rest of the girls were speechless. The sound of Pam's high-heeled boots clicking against the polished floor of the upstairs hall died in the distance before any of them could react.

"Jealous!" Katrina commented in a disgusted tone.

"Aren't we all!" Kay admitted with a laugh. Then she reached out and hugged Leah. "I'm glad you got the part, even though it's strange there's been no audition."

"Why audition?" Mia said coolly. "Without Alex around, Leah's a shoo-in these days for all of the good parts."

"Wrong!" Finola and Linda chimed in at once. Linda went on. "Lots of people get parts around here—Kay's had her turn being Clara in Patrick's *Nutcracker,* and Katrina won the Louise Adams Competition last fall. Alex was here then, too. And Leah's won and lost competitions and auditions, just like any one of us."

Mia frowned but backed down. She grudgingly held a hand out to Leah. "I can't say I feel good about this," the second-year student allowed as the girls marched together up the stairs. "But I know you can do it, so good luck!"

"And one and two and turn, arabesque. Leah, châîné into the wings," Madame Preston ordered. It was past five, and the first rehearsal for *Dance Indigo* should have been over twenty minutes ago.

Leah obediently kept turning, focusing on her spot, the silver-painted heat pipe sizzling against the studio wall. Leah châînéed past the strip of masking tape on the floor that marked where the opera-house stage ended and the wings began, before she came off pointe. Grabbing her towel off the barre, Leah mopped the sweat off her face and shoulders and watched as Madame went on rehearsing Patrick Hogan and Ashley Phillips.

Madame's sharp voice rose above the cough of the pipes as she barked instructions to her other dancers. "Ashley, keep circling Patrick ... arms softer ... no." Madame clapped her hands and the piano stopped. "Like this, Ashley, like this! Remember, *Dance Indigo* has a story. Each gesture of your arm, your head, your eyes must suggest a meaning. At this moment you are trying to seduce Patrick, to steal him from Leah, and you think—because she is off in the wings—that you have succeeded." The gray-haired teacher sprang up on three-quarter pointe and demonstrated the pirouettes and the correct port de bras to the ballerina. Even in tailored black pants and a soft pink sweater, sixty-year-old Madame managed to make the steps look youthful and sensual.

Ashley followed right behind Madame, marking the steps. She was a round, slightly chubby dancer dressed in ratty black knit tights, a stretched-out beige leotard, and rather broken-down black leather pointe shoes. When Leah had first seen the fresh-faced, freckled young woman, she couldn't imagine why Madame had chosen her for the second girl's part in *Dance Indigo*. Now, watching her dance, Leah was spellbound. Even in the unglamorous atmosphere of the cramped, brightly lit North Studio, Ashley gave the impression of moonlight dancing on the ocean. She was also the sexiest dancer Leah had ever seen—perfectly cast for the part of the vamp.

Madame paused to check with Sue Cohen, the

company choreologist, to be sure that she was following the carefully notated steps. Then Madame motioned for the accompanist to continue with the Dvořák score. "Leah," she called out over her shoulder, "why don't you take a ten-minute break? I want to work through this passage with Patrick and Ashley, then we'll go right into the pas de trois we rehearsed earlier."

With a towel draped over her shoulders, Leah skirted the mirrored wall and headed for the barre at the back of the room, near where she had tossed her dance gear. She flopped down on the floor beneath the barre and closed her eyes for a moment. Then she fished a pair of purple leg warmers and a blue cardigan out of her bag and shrugged into them before her muscles had a chance to get cold. She leaned back against the wall, absently toying with the slightly frayed drawstring of a small, black-beaded sack. Alex's grandmother had made it when Alex was a little girl and first left home to board at the Leningrad Ballet School. The precious bag had held Alexandra's first pair of satin blocked toe shoes, and she had carried it all the way to America when she was twelve years old and her parents had defected.

The night before she left the Academy, Alex had presented the treasured bag to Leah, her face wet with tears. Now Leah looked down at it and wished that the bag still belonged to Alex and that Alex had never left. Leah longed to go back to the boardinghouse tonight, knock on Alex's door, and tell her every detail of today's rehearsal. Without Alex to share her doubts or successes, they just didn't seem real.

"Stephenson!" Madame called from the front of the studio, and Leah looked up, guilty that she hadn't been following Patrick and Ashley's progress at all.

"Let's get back to work now. Take it from your entrance in the pas de trois. Ashley, you'd be farther downstage at this point."

Leah stripped off her leg warmers and tossed her cardigan onto the barre. She hitched up the strap of her rose-red unitard, kicked out a kink in her knee, then nodded to the accompanist. Leah smiled at Patrick from the taped-off wings, then ran into the opening lift of the pas de trois.

"No, Leah, like this!" Madame corrected, and the music stopped.

She stepped in front of Leah to do the sequence herself. Patrick easily slipped his hands around Madame's slim waist, and she demonstrated the position of the head and arms. "Look over your shoulder like this." She turned her head and looked up into Patrick's eyes. "For you the angle of the neck will be different—you are on pointe and you are also a little shorter than I am."

Leah couldn't believe her eyes. A moment ago Madame had shown Ashley how to look more seductive, and now she was every inch the innocent young girl in love for the first time. Leah tried the combination again. Stepping cautiously into Patrick's arms, she put her hands up in a startled gesture and let him lift her just far enough so that she seemed to be floating next to him rather than walking.

"Excellent, Leah, excellent. Look surprised now

and a little afraid. Pretend you're a girl who's never been kissed before."

Patrick kept dancing, but he laughed at Madame's reflection in the mirror. "Maybe she doesn't have to pretend no one's kissed her yet, Madame." He winked at Leah as he spun her in a slow supported turn. "She's only fifteen!"

Madame actually chuckled, and behind Leah, Ashley giggled. But Leah wasn't laughing. Tears came to her eyes as she remembered how she had felt the first time she kissed Peter, just three weeks ago. The startled gesture, the turn of her head, and the half-smile on her lips were real for Leah, and her performance obviously pleased Madame.

"Perfect!" Madame clapped her hands. She motioned for Robert to stop the music one more time and to start from the top again. "Let's keep that feeling. Patrick, quit grinning; you'll put Leah in the wrong mood."

This time Leah felt a little stiff and almost started the third supported turn on the wrong foot. Patrick skillfully corrected her, and Madame didn't stop the rehearsal again. She went on to Ashley's entrance.

Once more Leah was impressed, and humbled. Ashley only needed to see Madame demonstrate a step once before copying it perfectly. In fact, both Ashley and Patrick seemed to catch on to the whole feeling of the dance much faster than Leah. All at once she felt incredibly young and inexperienced. In spite of this chance to enter the professional world, Leah had to remind herself that she was still just a student.

After one final run-through, Madame broke up the rehearsal for the day. "We'd better quit while we're ahead. Patrick has to get ready for a performance tonight at the Opera House—as do you, Ashley. I hear you're filling in in *Jewels* for Diana."

"In 'Diamonds,' yes, I am. It's on the program first and I have to wear *all* that makeup. And that dumb tiara keeps vanishing in my hair every time I try to get it pinned on right! It takes forever to get my costume organized." She babbled something about a fitting, then, with a brief apologetic bow in Madame's direction, hurried over to Patrick and planted a friendly kiss on his cheek.

"As always, a pleasure dancing with you, my dear!" she chirped in a birdlike voice. "And a nice piece, *Indigo*. Strong feeling but easy dancing, I think. Don't you?" While she talked, she yanked the elastic out of her hair and shook out a mass of red-gold curls.

Patrick nodded. "A real little masterpiece," he commented. "Madame, as always, is full of surprises! And at least it'll be one part of Wednesday's program we don't have to sweat through." They arranged to have coffee together before that night's performance, then Ashley waved good-bye to Leah.

"Great meeting you, Leah! This is super fun working together."

"Good work, Leah," Patrick told her on his way out the door. "I'm pretty impressed with you!" He yelled good-bye to Robert, then headed for the men's changing room. Leah looked sadly after him. Ashley and Patrick were going off to put in a night's work performing and Leah was left behind.

Worse, Leah didn't feel that good about her work at all, especially after the other dancers had said the piece was easy. Leah had found the dancing hard. At the moment all she could remember was how many times Madame had had to repeat her instructions or correct her line or modify her timing of the steps. Madame was probably regretting her decision to use Leah at all. Leah reached for her towel and draped it over her head to pat the sweat off her face.

"Do you like the ballet?" Madame asked suddenly, arriving at her side.

Leah whipped the towel away and faced Madame. "Like it?" she squeaked. She clasped her hands in front of her. "Oh, Madame, it's such a beautiful ballet—but ..." Leah couldn't bring herself to voice her fears out loud.

"Good," Madame interrupted in her usual brusque manner. "I felt this piece would suit you—you are the same sort of dancer as Diana. You have the same body type."

Leah didn't know how to respond to that. Because it was true: Leah and Diana Chang fit into the exact same costumes, had the same strong but lyrical quality of movement, a perfect sense of balance, a pure classical style. Diana, however, wasn't a student. She taught at the school and was currently the Bay Area Ballet's brightest young ballerina. She had recognized Leah's ability right off the bat and considered the fifteen-year-old girl a threat to her own career. More than once Diana had made life pretty unpleasant for Leah, in class and around the school in general. These days Leah was very careful what she said to anyone—even

Madame—about Diana Chang. Leah took a deep breath, and when she could trust her voice, she replied, "Yes, I heard she was originally cast in this."

"You're right. Actually, the revival of *Dance Indigo* was intended as a vehicle for her. Now that she's starring in *Temptations* she can't do it. The shoots interfere with her whole performing schedule this season." Madame's voice was tight when she said that, and Leah bit her lip. Originally the film part had been offered to Leah, who was really a fifteen-year-old student like Cara Dean, the movie's fictional heroine. That was a fact that had appealed to the producer as much as her photo in a magazine spread that had caught his attention had. But Leah, to Madame's great relief, had turned the offer down, feeling that she had too much to learn at the school and as a performer to risk a break in her education at this point in her life.

"But don't worry about how Diana would dance this ballet," Madame was saying. "Just give it your best, Leah. I think you will develop the role nicely, in your own way." Madame walked back to the piano to confer with Robert. "That was a very credible first rehearsal, Leah. Considering you've never done this kind of work before, you're a surprisingly quick study," she said, leaving Leah stunned.

For five seconds Leah stood planted in the center of the floor, just staring at Madame's back. Then the hall clock chimed and Leah remembered that she was already late for the top-secret students-only meeting in the library. She hurried across the studio, grabbed her things, and ducked into the dressing room for a quick change of clothes.

Maybe Alex wasn't around for her to talk to, Leah thought as she looked at herself in the mirror, but she would always remember the things Alex had told her. Alex had always said that Leah worried too much. As usual, Alex was right.

Just when Leah had been feeling like the most uncoordinated person in the world, Madame had complimented her on her work.

After a day's worth of dancing and rehearsing, Leah was bursting with newfound energy. And this was just the beginning of her professional career—the best was yet to come!

Chapter 3

"Ta-dah-da-dah-da-dah!" Kenny Rotolo greeted Leah with a flourish when she poked her head into the small library.

Leah looked quickly around the crowded room and spotted Finola perched on the librarian's desk. Leah cast her an apologetic glance. According to the clock on the wall, she was forty minutes late. "Sorry," Leah murmured, trying to climb over everyone and find a place to sit down. "Rehearsal ran late!" she explained.

"What was it like?" Linda asked as Leah made her way to the one square foot of space Kay had saved for her on the rubber mat in front of the reference desk. "Is it really tough working so closely with Madame?"

"What's Ashley Phillips like?" another voice asked. "I've never seen her."

"No one has—she's been guesting abroad!" Kay informed the crowd.

The barrage of questions made Leah laugh. "I've always wanted to know what a press conference felt like," she said, poking her chin up in the air and trying to look every bit the international ballet star. Kay let out a hearty laugh. "But my agent won't let me talk right now!" Leah shrugged sheepishly and basked in the laughter that followed her remark. She dropped into a deep curtsy in front of her friends, then Kay pulled her down beside her on the floor. After the intense workout with Ashley, Patrick, and Madame, Leah felt great being back with her fellow students. She elbowed Kay and took a tortilla chip out of the small bag she was holding. She'd been too nervous for lunch and now felt like she was starving. "Any more where these came from?" She rattled the bag under Kay's nose.

"Here you go!" Kenny tossed an apple in Leah's direction, and she toasted him with it before she took her first bite. She savored her snack for a moment, then turned to Kay.

"I'm glad it's over for today," she confided in an undertone just as Finola banged one of her shoes on the desk to bring the meeting back to order. Kay looked like she was dying to hear more, but Leah put a finger to her lips and pointed to Finola.

"I'm sorry you're late, Leah, because you are just going to have to accept your assignment." From the twinkle in Finola's eyes Leah had a feeling that she had been appointed to dance something very silly. "It *is* a solo, though!"

"As long as I get to wear a tutu!" Leah called out. Several of the other girls groaned in sympathy. All of Leah's solo stints this year—including her big performance in a fund-raising gala with famous Russian dancer Andrei Levintoff as her partner—had been danced in long, flowing dresses or in unitards. Only once since she'd come to the school had she performed in the costume of her dreams, a fluffy brocade-and-tulle tutu.

"Oh, you'll wear a tutu for this one!" Finola smiled evilly, and Leah winced, dreading the outfit Finola had in mind.

A loud cackle came from Kenny's general direction, but someone clapped a hand over his mouth, and the room settled back down into relative silence.

Finola checked the clipboard in her hands, then finally announced, "You have been chosen—"

"Mainly because you're blond!" Pam interrupted.

Finola ignored Pam's comment and went on, "to dance ... ta-da! Drum roll, please ... *The Dead Chicken!*"

A chorus of various fowllike squawks and clucks followed Finola's announcement. Leah doubled over at the joke. "That's funny," she said when the laughter died down, "but what am I *really* dancing?"

"The Dead Chicken!" the whole room seemed to answer in unison.

"It's a parody of *The Dying Swan,*" Finola quickly explained. "Someone choreographed it ages ago at my school in London. I danced it once—with a wig one of the senior boys borrowed from the company store." She grinned at the memory.

"The Dead Chicken!" Leah repeated, horrified. "I will not dance in anything like that. I won't!" A deep blush stained her face and it took every ounce of willpower not to scramble to her feet and march right out of the overheated, over-

crowded basement library. She felt as if her life as a dancer had just plunged from the sublime to the ridiculous. One minute she was a budding star in a company production, the next minute a goofy schoolgirl aping a famous ballerina in a parody of *The Dying Swan*. Leah wasn't even going to bother to point out that dead chickens, in any case, certainly didn't dance.

"Leah's just being a snob as usual," Pam said, buffing her glossy scarlet nails against her peacock-blue shirt. "I mean, a solo's good enough for everyone else around here."

Leah glared at Pam. "Give it up, Pam," she snapped. Beside her, Kay whispered a cheer.

Kay studied Leah's face and frowned a little. "You aren't serious about not liking the ballet though, are you? You can't be. Finola danced it herself once at a gala at the Royal Ballet School, and she said it's a real hoot, and hard work, too. Finola said it would be perfect for you. You do the best dying swan in the whole school."

"Birds of a different feather," Leah muttered. She hadn't meant that to be a joke, but everyone around her started to laugh.

"I wasn't trying to be funny," Leah protested, but her voice didn't carry over the noise in the room. She stretched out her legs; they were beginning to cramp up after the strenuous rehearsal, and whatever energy she'd felt an hour before seemed to have suddenly fizzled out. Dinner was what she needed, dinner and a very hot, very long bubble bath. Quiet time, to digest everything she'd learned during rehearsal so that next time she wouldn't mess up at all in front of Madame. Suddenly, being with her friends didn't feel quite as great as it had ten minutes ago. "Don't you think Madame deserves something a little more serious?" Leah asked, trying the rational approach.

"The idea of this gala is *not* to be serious!" Finola pointed out. "What if we changed the title?" she suggested. "Would that make you feel better?"

"How about *The Plucked Chicken?*" Kenny called out.

Mia practically choked on the apple she was eating. When she recovered, she said, *"Homage to Kentucky Fried."* The room was filled with hoots and screams and loud clucking sounds.

Leah rolled her eyes. She was losing patience with the entire meeting. Suddenly, even the idea of a student evening for Madame seemed childish. "I think Madame deserves better than a spoof of *The Dying Swan* for her birthday," she observed.

"But she isn't just getting a spoof, Leah!" Kay cried. "Not at all. My piece will be an original creation."

"You can say that again," Pam quipped.

"Oh, shut up, Pam." Michael Litvak leapt to Kay's defense. Then he turned to face Leah. "The point is, we need someone strong for the solo part, someone who can act—"

"And who's blond!" someone reminded him from over by the periodical shelves.

"Right!" Finola said. "I'd do it myself, but I can't. I can't run the whole gala, get the costumes together, do the lights, and make the sets!" The usually calm Finola actually sounded frazzled, and

Leah could see she'd have to give in. She didn't want to let her friends down.

"All right, I'll dance it, I'll dance it," she told the room.

A chorus of cheers met her decision. Then Michael, who had been voted Finola's second-in-command, began rounding up volunteers for building sets.

Finola had been watching Leah carefully, and as soon as Kay bounced off to schedule rehearsals with her dancers, she tapped Leah on the shoulder. "But . . . ?"

Leah looked up. "Well . . ." She didn't want to sound like a snob about her solo, but something else was bothering her, too. There was no point in trying to fool Finola. The English girl wasn't like Alex at all, but she had the same worldly, experienced air about her, as if she were older than seventeen. "I feel silly dancing in front of Madame in something so . . . undignified the night before I do *Indigo.*"

To Leah's surprise, Finola looked sympathetic. "In your shoes I might feel the same way," Finola mused. "But Madame will probably love it *and* . . ." Finola looked positively conniving for a moment. "I think it'll be good for your image around this place. You'll look more versatile."

Leah hadn't thought of that at all.

Finola sat back on her heels and pondered. "The one criticism I've ever heard about your dancing—though I've only heard it once or twice and I'm not sure I agree—is that you're a little too stiff and classical."

Leah sighed. "The time I danced with Andrei, the critic in the *Chronicle* said that."

"Well, he said you had the makings of a great dancer, too. But I think something like *The Dead Chicken*—" Leah winced, and Finola rushed on. "I think performing it on a stage will be good for you."

Leah digested Finola's comment, then started to smile. "You don't have to convince me. I said I'd do it, and I will. But now at least I won't feel so dumb about it." Leah studied her hands and frowned. Lately she'd taken to biting her nails again, something she hadn't done since she was ten.

Finola followed her glance. "Something else is bothering you." She stretched her legs out and prepared herself to listen to Leah's problem.

Leah met Finola's eyes and tried to put her feelings into words. "I guess I don't like the idea of only dancing alone. Part of the fun of the gala is working with everyone—and a solo means you more or less work alone. And besides, I wanted to do more. Even *The Dying Swan* can't take very long." Leah rubbed her arms. "I almost can't get enough dancing these days to keep me busy."

"And keep your mind off Alex," Finola said softly. "You don't have to prove anything, Leah. You won't leave—you're not like Alex. You're going to stick it out."

Leah's head snapped up. "I didn't say anything about leaving!" she retorted, a little too quickly.

Finola held Leah's glance, then shrugged. "Well, you've certainly got a lot on your shoulders. If I were you, I'd be feeling a little mixed up."

"I'm not mixed up," Leah insisted. "I just want to work harder on this gala. I feel like I want to do more—for Madame." Even as Leah said the words, she realized how important it was to show Madame, at the gala, as well as during the rehearsals for *Indigo* and of course at the company performances, how strong she was, how much she could do. She wouldn't let Madame down!

"She's done so much for me lately," Leah concluded, speaking almost to herself. Then she remembered Finola was listening and she felt embarrassed, as if she really were the teacher's pet, like Pam said. "Sounds silly, doesn't it?' she asked shyly.

"No, it makes sense. So let's see what else I can give you." Finola riffled through her papers. "But I don't think we should have another pas de deux ... hmm, something with other people in it that could make use of you." Finola scanned the yellow sheets of paper and frowned. "I don't know what's left for you to do with a group. I know you don't have time to help with costumes, and you're not exactly a great seamstress." Finola tried to be tactful. "I somehow can't quite picture you painting sets."

Leah was notorious for her rather beautiful but incredibly sloppy painting in art class.

Finola sat for a moment with her legs out at a 180-degree angle, her elbows on the floor, staring blankly at her notes. She chewed the eraser end of her pencil, waiting for inspiration to strike. Suddenly, her face lit up. "Got it!" she shouted, and bounded to her feet.

Leah must have looked startled, because Finola

beamed down at her and let out a laugh that was pure music. "Around SFBA one must never, ever forget about Kay!" Then she dusted off the back of her black cropped stretch pants and set off to find the short, dark-haired girl.

Seconds later she and Kay returned. "Kay agrees," Finola declared, smiling.

"In fact, I think it's a brilliant idea," Kay said, leaving Leah in the dark a moment longer.

"What?" Leah asked, not quite in the mood for guessing games. "Kay, what are you talking about?"

"If you want, you can work with me, too," Kay said.

Leah was mystified.

"In my ballet, though it won't be a ballet exactly," she warned. "But I should have thought of it myself. You'd be perfect. I have just the part in mind."

"No chicken feathers?" Leah began to smile.

"No, nothing like that!" Kay sounded scornful. Her choreography was something she took very seriously. After all, Andrei himself had once said that Kay had the makings of a really great choreographer.

Leah thought for a moment. The gala was the day before her big company premiere. But somehow the prospect of hard work suited her. Not just hard work, but hard work with one of her best friends. "I'd love it," she said a bit fiercely. "I think it would be fun."

Finola penned in Leah's name at the bottom of the list for Kay's ballet. "That's going to be a lot of work," she said slowly. "It's a great idea and all, but aren't you going to be stretching yourself a bit too thin?"

"Work is what I feel like right now," Leah said confidently. "I can do it, Finola. Trust me. I've got a great idea: we can call your parody *The Sick Chicken!*"

"They still manage to move around!" Kay giggled and lapsed into an imitation of a droopy bird.

"I love it!" Finola smiled at Leah, who grinned back. All at once the pieces of her life seemed to be falling into place: being cast in *Indigo* by Madame, making her professional debut, once again working closely with really good friends. Suddenly, the hole left by Alex and Peter didn't seem so big anymore.

"Yes," Leah repeated, and jumped to her feet. She pirouetted into the hall and back again. "I'm going to love working with my friends!"

Chapter 4

The next morning Leah got up at the crack of dawn. A thin sliver of gold shone through the bathroom window as she stood in front of the sink splashing cold water on her face.

She toweled herself off, then paused only long enough to watch the day begin. Today, she thought, starts the first day of the rest of my life. She had read that somewhere, but the words suddenly rang very true. Just yesterday Leah had left her room for school, a student training to be a dancer; today she was beginning the first full day of her professional life.

Leah tiptoed down the front stairs and into the kitchen. Her young cat Misha brushed against her leg, mewing for some milk. "Here, boy," she said, pouring him a bowlful. He was hungry, but Leah didn't have time to search the pantry for the cat food. "Someone will be up later to feed you," she assured Misha, patting him quickly on the head. Then, grabbing an apple and her books, she slipped on her blue jacket and hurried out the front door just as Mrs. Hanson's alarm went off.

Leah could barely stop herself from running the quarter mile from the boardinghouse to the school. But since jogging was bad for a dancer's ankles and knees, she forced herself to settle for a very fast walk. She drank in the fresh morning air and tried to ignore the empty feeling in her stomach. Leah often woke up ravenous and usually ate a good-sized breakfast, but today dancing seemed more important than food.

She bypassed the front gate and went across the school parking lot to the side entrance of the main building, which was already open. One of the maintenance men looked up from his sweeping and said good morning as Leah started up the short, broad flight of steps. Through an open third-floor window, the sound of someone practicing the piano floated on the cool breeze. Leah allowed herself a moment more of sunlight, then plunged into the dark school. She passed the Academy offices, all still closed. It was almost seven-thirty. She had just enough time to go to the library before her morning class and study the thirty-year-old file film of the original production of *Dance Indigo*. Happily she skipped downstairs.

An hour and a half later, Leah's eyes were drooping with fatigue. Never again would she leave Mrs. Hanson's without breakfast or at least a cup of strong tea. She was yawning as she walked into the sumptuous second-floor Red Studio.

"Watch your step, Goldilocks!" a gruff voice commanded. Then a calloused hand grabbed her elbow, just as she almost tripped over a bundle of thick cables taped to the studio floor.

Leah's eyes popped open. The man who had saved her from a nasty fall was about twenty years old and was very cute. But Leah's eyes were fixed on the pink *Temptations* logo on his black T-shirt. "What's going on here?" she asked, stepping back. She took in the cables, which were carefully placed along the back of the room where no one danced; the large trunks stashed alongside Robert's grand piano; the two movie cameras up in the front corner near the window; the bank of heavy-duty lights; and the dozen or so men and women in jeans, black shirts, and stockinged feet milling around the edges of the studio.

"*Temptations!* The filming starts today. Here!" Katrina informed Leah in quick, nervous sentences. Katrina retrieved a towel and some tissues from her dance bag, then shoved it into the pile near the rosin box. "Don't tell me you really forgot?" She checked her hair in the mirror and tucked the frizzy brown strands back into her thick, coiled braid. Flicking a dot of mascara off her lightly made-up face, she grinned at Leah.

Leah blushed and self-consciously pushed her hair back into her bun. In the midst of yesterday's confusion she really had forgotten about *Temptations.* And she had a feeling that being in a small part of the film she was supposed to have starred in was not going to be a pleasant experience. "No, I didn't forget exactly. I just didn't remember filming was scheduled to start here today."

Leah frowned. She looked as neat and well-groomed as she always did for Madame's class, but if she'd remembered about the cameras being there that morning she would have done something special with her hair or even wore a new black leotard. She didn't even have a drop of makeup on. She scanned the front of the room and let out a dismal little groan. The film's handsome producer, Clark Rees, was already there talking to a bearded man with a hat. Leah didn't want him to see her looking so drab.

"I think you *wanted* to forget!" Pam commented shrewdly. She dropped down onto the floor a few feet from Leah and started to warm up.

"Since when are you the amateur psychologist around here?" Linda scoffed.

"If Leah had played her cards right, she'd be the star of the class today, not Diana Chang," Pam pointed out. She lowered her voice. "I caught a glimpse of Diana. They've turned the small girls' dressing room at the other end of the hall into a makeup studio. She looks ..." Pam stopped to laugh at her recollection. "Shall we say, very immature!"

Leah tuned out Pam and Linda's conversation and dropped down onto the floor to begin her own series of warmups. Perhaps if she hadn't just gotten the part in *Dance Indigo* she'd be more flustered about having to be just an extra in the feature-length ballet film. But today her decision to stick with SFBA seemed to be the right one.

"Leah Stephenson, are you deaf, or what!" Katrina demanded. Leah realized Katrina had called her name several times.

Leah's head jerked up. She had actually dozed off in the middle of her stretches. Annoyed with herself, she snapped at Katrina, "Of course not. I'm working."

"Oh!" Pam spoke up from the barre nearby. "I thought you had just turned into an instant snob."

"Leah's dancing at that matinee is not going to turn her into a snob," Finola chided, poking some hairpins into her thick French braid.

"I agree, Finola. *Dance Indigo* isn't the problem," Pam said with a bored yawn. "Being a little girl's idol, though, may be. That probably went right to her head!" she commented, looking disdainfully at Leah. "Or maybe you all haven't heard the big news yet?"

Pam paused dramatically and cleared her throat. "Leah's got a fan!" she announced, loudly enough for several heads to turn at the news.

Leah felt herself blush. She got up and dusted off her tights, then squeezed past Pam to her assigned place at the barre.

"After the company performance," Finola said sharply. "Leah's going to have lots of fans, Pam. And you're just jealous." The English girl motioned for Katrina to join her at the barre across the room, but not before Kay burst in, late as usual. She looked excitedly from the film crew to the cameras, then ran over to the other girls.

"I forgot to tell you guys yesterday! Did you hear?" Kay exclaimed. "Sophie Potter, *the* Sophie Potter, is living in Alex's room!" She paused to catch her breath. Then hopping first on her right foot and then on her left, she struggled to slip on her pink-leather ballet slippers.

Finola's dark eyebrows arched slightly. "The girl who won the Moscow competition?" she asked.

"She's coming here? But I thought she was just a kid," Katrina put in. "I saw an article in *Dance-*

Magazine about her. She's, like, twelve or something."

Pam frowned. "Really, Kay, you have a way of spoiling the best stories." The redhead stomped back over to the barre and took her usual place right behind Leah. "The point is, our little Sophie has a crush on Leah."

For the first time since she was eight years old, Leah had an urge to punch another girl in the nose. Her anger must have showed because, after a quick warning look, Linda came to her rescue.

"Translation!" Linda said loud enough for the whole room to hear. "She recognized Leah from her picture in *FootNotes* and was eager to meet her! I think that's great. It proves that in spite of being a so-called prodigy, the kid's not a snob."

"No one said Sophie's the snob around here!" Pam complained.

As it turned out, Pam got the last word. Madame walked into the room just then and clapped her hands together sharply.

"Good morning, girls!" she said as the dancers scurried to their places at the barres. "I have an announcement of sorts."

"Sophie!" Pam whispered from her spot behind Leah.

"The movie, dummy," Linda whispered hoarsely.

"Diana!" Kay's comment was definitely too loud. Then the door leading from the dressing room slammed and everyone turned around. Diana Chang had walked in and she was dressed in regulation SFBA clothes. Leah couldn't believe it: Company dancers never turned up for class like that, not even for Madame's. Leah's eyes went from Diana's obviously new pink tights to her long-sleeved black leotard to the white elastic tie around her tiny waist. Leah had never seen Diana wear so much makeup to class. Her dark eyes were heavily lined and her cheeks were brushed with a dusky blush.

Leah wasn't the only one who noticed Diana's unusual outfit. Excited comments buzzed around the room.

Madame rapped her hand sharply on the back of the high stool. "Silence, please!"

Leah put one hand on the barre and drew her back up very straight. She stared straight ahead and scarcely dared to breathe until every last whisper in the room had died down. Madame was clearly in a bad mood.

"There is already too much disruption around the school today. As I'm sure you are well aware, filming of *Temptations* starts this morning here at the Academy." Before anyone could say anything, Madame held up her hand. "I would appreciate your complete attention. Now, in spite of all this equipment cluttering our studio and the halls of the school in general, this is first and foremost a serious school of dance, not a movie set. I expect all of my students to work as if nothing out of the ordinary is happening."

Leah hazarded a glance at Madame. Today her hair was drawn back into a tight chignon, and she looked as stern as always. Still, Leah thought she detected the slightest hint of a smile in her eyes. Obviously Madame was perfectly aware that her girls were no more capable of ignoring the film crew than they would be of ignoring a UFO that suddenly descended into the middle of the class-room.

Madame took a deep breath and went on. "The third floor will be off-limits to all students for the next three days."

Several groans greeted this announcement. All of the practice pianos and music rooms were on the top floor, and several dancers at the school also studied an instrument. Besides, every time a part of the Academy was put off-limits, for whatever reason, rehearsal and class schedules tended to get hopelessly confused.

When the complaints died down, Madame continued. "Today, a small crew, including the film's producer, Clark Rees ..." Madame paused here and bowed toward the back of the room. Leah turned around with the others and blushed when the handsome producer smiled right at her. He had desperately wanted Leah for the starring role, but he had also understood her reasons for turning down his offer. Leah had found him an interesting man and thought of him as a friend.

"Mr. Rees's company will be shooting some class footage. Now, I am told it is very important for the purposes of the movie that you girls *ignore* the camera. For the purposes of this class, I expect your attention—as usual—to be one hundred and ten percent on your dancing."

The silver-haired teacher paused for a moment, then said in a quiet, firm voice, "Do you understand?"

"Yes, Madame," everyone answered, sounding just as scared as Leah felt.

"Then we'll begin." Madame gestured to Robert,

then turned to Clark Rees. "Where do you want Diana?"

Her gaze landed right at Leah's spot, the place of honor at the front of the barre on the right. Leah had inherited the spot when Alex had left, to the chagrin of the older students. But Mr. Rees quickly consulted with a bearded man standing next to him, who shook his head. Behind him was a chair marked DIRECTOR.

"It is important Diana looks like an ordinary student," the director said with a heavy German accent. "Not like the best in the class."

When Pam muttered "Fat chance!" Leah couldn't help but agree. Diana was a very professional and gifted dancer. She'd make everyone in the class look bad.

Diana was finally placed between Kay and Mia on the other side of the room. Someone fiddled a moment with the lights, then the music started. Leah forced her eyes off Diana's reflection in the mirror and tried to concentrate on her pliés. She wanted to dance the best barre she could. Perhaps the camera was focused on Diana, but Leah was aware that she herself had been first to star in this film.

And she didn't want Mr. Rees to forget that fact. She wanted him to think she was still equal to the part, even if she had turned it down. Above all, she didn't want to disappoint Madame.

The *whirr* of the cameras clicking on and off was distracting at first, until Madame began shouting her usual corrections.

"Fanny down, Leah." "Pam, get those knees over those feet!" "Sondra, what are you doing with that arm? You look like a scarecrow, not a balle- rina." "Linda, mind your own business, please, and Kay, we dance with our feet around here, not our mouths!"

The last comment cracked the class up, but Leah didn't let herself laugh. Laughing seemed so unprofessional, and today Leah had pledged her- self to begin her life as a professional dancer.

Madame was right. Their business here was to dance, to give over one hundred percent of them- selves. She forced herself to pay attention to her own body. She allowed the music to fill her and tried to dance her way through barre work, the way she had seen Patrick and Ashley dance their way through rehearsal yesterday, not worrying about every step. At the same time, she was keenly aware of how each muscle in her body was work- ing. How, during tendus, her arch stretched out to its fullest, then, as she drew her foot back to fifth position, it relaxed for an instant. Never be- fore had Leah gone through a barre with such a focused mind *and* body.

When Madame spoke, Leah practically jumped. "Excellent barre, Leah. Excellent. I think at last something very good is happening inside here." Madame patted Leah's head as she walked by to take her position for center work.

Leah was too shocked even to smile. It was the first time Madame had given Leah such an out- right compliment in class.

It was Kay who put it best later, when the girls were at the back of the room changing for pointe work. "You were better, Leah. You were better than Diana!" Kay sounded awed.

"You weren't supposed to watch Diana!" Finola lightly bopped Kay on the head with one of her shoes. "But you're right."

"So you watched, too," Pam said snidely, but she stared hard at Leah.

Leah, in turn, was staring at Kay. "Better than Diana?" She sounded surprised. Then she gave an embarrassed little laugh. "I forgot all about her."

"You what!" five voices said at once. Katrina looked past Leah to the hallway into which Diana had disappeared. Apparently the crew wasn't shooting footage of pointe work this morning, and as soon as the center work was over, Diana, accompanied by Mr. Rees and the camera crew, had quit the room.

Leah shrugged. "I really forgot she was here."

Pam snickered. "Pity she won't forget you!"

Leah cringed a little. Unfortunately, what Pam said was true. Diana had still been in the room when Madame had complimented her. More fuel for Diana's fire, Leah thought ruefully, then pushed the thought right out of her head. With Diana busy making a movie and Leah filling in for her at the Opera House, there wasn't much damage even a furious Diana Chang could do!

Chapter 5

An hour later an argument began in art class. Mr. Hart, the painting teacher, had set up a still life and then left for the day, so everyone was doing a lot of talking and very little painting.

"I think it was insulting, humiliating, and completely unnecessary to have a professional dancer in class with us pretending to be a student. He should have been in the company boys' class, not here at the school," Marc Gatineau, a new student from Quebec, argued. The five-foot-ten, blue-eyed dancer daubed angrily at the canvas with his brush. Red paint splattered all over the floor, on the front of his coveralls, and onto the gold-wire frames of the glasses he wore whenever he wasn't dancing. "And of all people, James Cummings! I mean all you girls, in Madame's class, at least are up to a level of good corps work. But we boys, we ..." He hesitated, then lapsed into a string of French expressions that no one could understand.

Kay took pity on the handsome, dark-haired boy and gently tried to explain the situation. "I guess being new here at the school you didn't realize exactly what you were getting into. But classes are always being disrupted for one thing or another. Of course, none of us have had to work with a film crew watching us before."

"Arrrgh!" Marc made a dismissive gesture with his hands. "I do not care about the crew that watches us, but I do care about the fact that I am on film, supposed to be the first boy leading people across the class during cabrioles and then two places behind me is this—this—Cummings man!"

Leah knew she shouldn't laugh, but James—a man? "He's your age, Marc. He's still young. It's not like he's Andrei Levintoff—at least not yet." She had meant to get across the fact that Marc was also a strong dancer. He had started studying ballet late, only two years ago in his native Quebec, and had arrived at the school two weeks ago on a scholarship. His technique was rough and his partnering still a horror, which was why Patrick had wisely paired him with strong, athletic Pam in pas de deux class. But he was every inch as gifted a dancer as James. Unfortunately, Marc took every word she said the wrong way.

And so did Kay. "That's not fair, Leah. *You* haven't seen James really dance, full-out, in months and months. He's getting brilliant reviews. Someone called him the first American Nureyev! He's a professional now, not a student like the rest of us. And he has lots of stage experience. He was headed for international stardom even before this film deal came up. Why, it was as bad for the guys having him in class today with all those cameras whirring as it was for us having Diana around to show us up. I think we can all understand exactly how Marc feels."

The other students in the room murmured agreement.

Leah made a small, annoyed sound. She flicked her hair off her shoulder, then shrugged. "I think you're being a bit overdramatic. Besides, Madame assured us that no one but Diana will be visible in the final film."

"Fat chance of that!" Linda commented. She looked up from her painting. "If we weren't going to show in the final print, they wouldn't have had to film Diana in a real Academy class. They could have shot her alone and done something fancy in the cutting room. No, they wanted the atmosphere of Madame, and of us—looking like fools next to her."

"Oh, but, Linda," Pam said sulkily, "*everyone* didn't look like a fool. Why, Madame said so herself! And there are some people in class who regard themselves as quite professional these days." Pam didn't look at Leah as she said this, but it was obvious whom she was talking about.

"Exactly what do you mean by that?" Leah got up from her chair and planted her paint-covered hands on her hips. Blue and green fingerprints stained her jeans, but she was too angry to care.

"Come on, Leah. You *were* the only girl in class to be complimented—and right in front of Diana, too. So, obviously having her there didn't bother you as much as it bothered ... other people," Finola commented.

Now it was Pam's turn to take offense. "I didn't say *I* was bothered!"

"No one said you did, Pam." Michael Litvak, always the peacemaker, tried to smooth things over. Turning to Leah, he asked, "What did Madame say, anyway? Patrick not only didn't compliment us, he actually put James down." Michael chuckled. "I suppose there was no soundtrack!"

Leah sighed. "It wasn't a big deal."

"Not a big deal!" Kay said, sniffing indignantly. "She told Leah that she was finally beginning to get her act together!"

"And that is a compliment?" Marc seemed amazed.

Pam arched her finely tweezed eyebrows. "Marc, you have to understand that Leah is the teacher's pet around here. Madame always gives her special consideration. What she meant was that Leah was better than her usual perfect self. She acted as if Leah, not Diana, was the star of the class."

Marc grinned. "No wonder everyone is jealous of you," he said to Leah.

"Everyone's jealous of everyone around here," Katrina insisted, trying to deflect Marc's comment on Leah's behalf.

"But not everyone around here is getting to perform with the company next week!" Pam said.

"Is getting to *what?*" several of the guys said at once.

Michael stared at Leah. "What's Pam talking about?"

"You haven't heard?" Leah was surprised.

"I'm surprised you weren't on the phone all night, Kay, breaking the big news to everyone," Pam said, almost accusingly.

"Well, all of the girls knew yesterday." Kay sounded hurt. She marched over to the sink and began to wash her brushes.

Michael, Mark, Kenny, and Sam Denmare all exchanged glances. "We're second-class citizens around here, always the last to know," Sammy said. He was a first-year student who hailed from the San Francisco area and still lived at home. He was in the regular dance program but was training to be a choreographer.

Leah smiled shyly at Michael and said, "I should have told you myself yesterday. I really thought the whole school knew by the time of Finola's meeting, but I guess everyone got sidetracked by the gala plans. I'm dancing with the company, in two weeks, in *Dance Indigo*. Diana had to drop the role because of the filming schedule. Madame said I was the same type and size as Diana. So there won't be a problem with the costumes." Leah wasn't sure why she added that last part, but she didn't want Michael and the other guys to get the impression that Leah had been given the part only because she was a favorite of Madame's.

"When were the auditions?" Kenny asked innocently.

"There were none!" Kay and Pam said in unison.

"Leah seemed the logical person," Finola added. "And without Alex around . . . I heard from Andrei that Madame had plans for Alex, but—"

Leah spun around on her chair. "What plans?" she asked a bit sharply. It was the first she'd heard of Madame really wanting to help Alex.

"I don't know," Finola admitted honestly. "And Andrei didn't seem to want to talk about it. He's still confused about Alex leaving, like we all are, I guess. He said something about Sophie, too. Except I didn't know it was Sophie when he talked to me last week."

"You mean that *Potter* child?" Pam said, as though she'd like to kill her.

Leah cracked up. "She's only about three years younger than you are!" Leah wished she'd kept her mouth shut when she saw the way Pam's green eyes flashed. "Really, Pam, she's not as much of a threat as you seem to think."

"Not a threat?" Pam sputtered. "Easy for you to say. The girl worships the ground you walk on. But you just wait, Leah. How are you going to feel when she begins competing with you for parts?"

Leah pictured the plain, shy little girl sitting at Mrs. Hanson's dining-room table drinking a glass of milk. She wasn't old enough to be a real dancer yet. Leah gave a careless shrug, then stepped back from her easel to view her painting.

"She's only twelve!" Kay spoke up. "I'm really getting sick of this. Every time someone new and talented walks into this school, there's instant paranoia. Sophie will get parts, just like the rest of us. She's supposed to be good. But that doesn't make her a threat."

Finola didn't agree. "She's supposed to be a prodigy. And she certainly must be unusual enough for Madame to let a girl that age come here."

"What's she look like?" Kenny asked.

"Why?" Kay teased. Then her round face dropped into a frown. "Gosh, she's smaller than me." She gave the five-foot-five boy a panicky look. "They might make you *her* partner."

"You and I, dear Kay, are made for each other. They'll never break us apart!" he vowed.

"She probably does weigh less than eighty pounds," Pam said, then emitted a longing sort of sigh.

"Take me to her!" Marc said, not very tactfully.

Pam treated him to her coldest stare, then marched over to a corner to sulk. "She has absolutely no figure!" she remarked finally.

"And is plain as can be!" Linda added.

Leah didn't want to hear any more. "What is this? A beauty contest? Sophie is a perfectly fine-looking person. She's young and gawky, but who knows what she'll look like in a couple of years? And Kay said she saw her dance on television and she was wonderful."

"She was lovely," Kay said. "She doesn't have quite enough weight on her, so she looks a little—I don't know—ghostlike when she moves."

"The perfect Giselle!" Michael sighed. "I saw a tape of Makarova when she was about eighteen dancing that role, and she looked downright transparent."

"Well, Sophie's not Makarova. She's just Sophie. I, for one, look forward to seeing her in class. I think she'll make it next Sunday to Madame's," Kay added.

"And by Sunday afternoon, after Sophie's performed for Madame, I think the Great Stephenson will be singing a different tune," Pam predicted.

"Speak for yourself, Hunter. I've got more important things to worry about than Sophie Potter showing me up in class." Leah grabbed some paper towels and swabbed down her work space. She put her canvas up on the studio painting racks, wishing she could walk right back to the main building and away from all this gossip. But she had to wait for Kay, Linda, Michael, and Marc to head for the first rehearsal of Kay's new ballet.

Leah stood for a moment, watching the other kids get back to their work. She kicked the toe of one of her high tops against the baseboard and suddenly felt desolate. Then she grabbed a chair and headed for the door. Kay looked up, her eyes questioning.

"The turpentine's getting to me," Leah lied. "I need some air." She dragged the chair down the hall and out the entrance to the building. Sitting down and tilting it back against the white stucco wall, Leah looked across the lawn and back up toward the dance studios. "I don't care how good Sophie is!" she murmured aloud. "I really don't." But even saying it out loud to herself twice, Leah wasn't quite convinced. No matter how many times she reminded herself of Madame Preston's advice, Leah couldn't help but feel that her chances to be a great ballerina would go up in smoke the minute someone more talented came along.

Madame had told her girls again and again, Don't worry about the other person in class. A dancer's business is to work with her own body, her own strengths, her own particular weak points. Paying attention to the other dancers, in the long run, only hurt a dancer. Madame had said that during audition week back in September and a hundred and one times since then.

But Leah still wasn't sure she believed her.

Chapter 6

"We're rehearsing here?" Leah cried.
Kay had led her little troupe of dancers into the gym where Mia Picchi, Tom Kennedy, and Lindsay Kohlmeier were already waiting.

"Why not?" Mia said, slipping sweatpants over her footless tights. "Besides, there's nowhere else, with the top floor off-limits. And we can't exactly prepare a surprise for Madame's gala right in front of Madame."

Leah looked around. She was seldom in the small gymnasium and hadn't actually seen it without its Nautilus and weight equipment. SFBA students generally didn't play sports, particularly the girls, as most athletic activities tended to develop the wrong muscles. The Olympic-size pool was the focus of most people's workouts, and of course the boys trained regularly with weights. They also indulged in some impromptu basketball games, and lately the French teacher had instituted a boys' soccer team. Leah had to admit the pedestrian-looking gym didn't exactly inspire her to kick up her feet and dance.

"But the floor ..." Leah had taken off her sneakers and was sliding across the polished surface in her socks. "It's so slick, and I didn't bring rosin."

"No rosin needed," Kay said. She was waiting for Michael to finish hooking up her portable tape recorder to the electrical outlet near the backstop. "Bare feet, Leah. I told you this wasn't exactly an ordinary ballet."

"Oh!" Leah thought for a moment. "No shoes?"

"No shoes," Lindsay said, holding up a bare foot in Leah's direction.

"I don't have my modern dance stuff with me." Actually, Leah hadn't even taken a modern dance class at the Academy yet. She was putting off both the required choreography and modern technique classes until her second year at the school. Leah wasn't looking forward to either, and as she had told Patrick the day she enrolled, they reminded her of eating something good for her that she didn't like, such as peas.

"Not to worry," Kay assured her. "Sweats will do, and a leotard or even just a T-shirt on top. In fact, I like it better when people don't dress so dance-class for my sessions."

"Don't dress so 'dance-class' for my sessions ..." Leah repeated the phrase silently and wondered what in the world was wrong with dressing so "dance-class." She ducked into the ladies' room and changed into her sweats—the same pair she'd worn for rehearsal yesterday with Madame. They were really grimy now, and Leah wanted to kick herself for forgetting to dump the sweatpants in the wash. Tonight she'd remember, but in the meantime Kay and company would have to put up with her sloppy appearance.

By the time Leah had finished changing, Kay had found her music. Leah had expected one of Kay's favorite experimental "new music" scores —or nonscores. Her last piece, called *Sounds,* had been performed at the school's autumn fund-raising gala at the Opera House. It was to the sounds of crickets and birds and waterfalls. Leah hadn't been in it, but she had found it extraordinarily beautiful. But apparently Kay's inspiration this time came from the band Talking Heads.

"Now we'll begin with some loosening-up exercises," Kay said. She put her hands in the pockets of an oversized cardigan sweater and motioned for Leah to join the other dancers lined up on the floor. "Let's all work on circular motions. Let the music inspire you, but dance against it if you want, not with it."

Kay started her head circling, slowly around and around as in a neck-loosening exercise. Leah expected the other kids to follow suit, but instead Mia dropped to the floor and began pivoting in a circle around her own arm.

Michael began spinning slowly, then faster and faster with his arms stretched out. It was a game Leah remembered from back home in San Lorenzo; she and her best friend Chrissy constantly played it outside on the grass. They'd whirl about until the sky was swirling above them and then they'd tumble onto the ground, laughing. It was a game Leah loved, but she had never dreamed of calling it dancing.

She watched Michael, transfixed. She had the strongest urge to laugh. But as she looked around, everyone in the room seemed so deadly serious.

"Leah?" Kay had stopped whatever she was doing. She approached Leah, her hands on her small, round hips.

"I—I'm a little lost," Leah admitted, then started to grin. "I thought we would start the session by dancing."

"We are dancing." Kay's voice was quiet, and no one but Leah heard her over the boom of the music. "I realize why you're lost. You've never taken Johnny Cullum's choreography class. Well, the idea is to let each dancer find his or her own sort of movement. Everyone gets to improvise for a few minutes. Then I add my own ideas. Just do what feels natural, that's all, but keep the idea of circling in mind."

Back home in the rec room that she had transformed into a miniature studio, with a mirror and a portable barre, Leah had often improvised steps to music. Sometimes she even made up little ballets to music in the confines of her small bedroom here. Ballet steps to Talking Heads music never occurred to her, but she'd give it a try. "I've got the idea, I think," she said, then sprang up on three-quarter pointe and began doing bourrées around the circumference of the floor. When she got tired of that, she reversed direction and did some piqué turns. She felt terribly silly because the throbbing, repetitive beat of the music didn't seem to relate to the steps she was performing. And her bare feet felt as if they were sticking to the floor.

"Leah, stop dancing and loosen up. Just move... as if you'd never studied an hour of dance in your whole life!" Kay called out.

Leah stumbled and came to a stop. "As if I what?"

"Move like a person, not a dancer." Kay tried to make her point clearer. "Think of something that makes circles and pretend you're it—like a . . . like a . . ."

Kay flashed a helpless glance toward Linda, who was walking around in a pattern of circles: first inscribing narrower and narrower ones, then ones that grew wider and wider like ripples in water. "Think of what goes round—like a dog chasing its tail."

"A hawk or an eagle hunting!" Michael suggested as he came to a stop.

"Helicopter blades!" Lindsay whooped and happily demonstrated.

Leah shook her head in disbelief. "What's this got to do with dancing?"

"Movement—all movement is dancing," Kay said with a slightly superior air. "That's what choreography—at least the kind that's worthwhile these days—is all about. Finding the dance in the ordinary things people do."

"Like pretending they're helicopters?" Leah scoffed. "Really, Kay, I thought this was a serious sort of piece you were putting together. I mean, why have *us* perform for Madame? We're trained dancers. You could just as well go down to the high school and get any old kid to perform this stuff." Leah looked down at the shorter girl and said firmly, "I think you should do something more appropriate for her birthday, something that shows off what we do best. Ballet . . . the kind of ballet she teaches us."

"Hey, this is Kay's dance piece, not yours, Leah. She has a right to do what she wants," Mia blurted out.

"Who put you in charge, anyway?" Linda asked grumpily. "I like Kay's idea."

It suddenly struck Leah that she didn't know the first thing about Kay's idea. Kay must have gone over the dance with the others while Leah was still changing. "I must have missed that—the idea part," she explained, not meaning to sound sarcastic, but her words had that effect.

"Leah, you're not doing me any favors by being in my piece! Finola said you wanted to work *with* other people, and I thought you'd have fun."

"Fun?" Leah said tightly. "I'm here to dance, not to have fun. Of course I want to work with you, but I'm not a mind-reader. You haven't explained anything to me yet."

Marc cleared his throat. "There is no time for this," he reminded them, tapping his watch. "We had only an hour to start with and now we have just forty-five minutes. I have a partnering class with Pam at one-thirty. And I know everyone here has a lot to do this afternoon."

Marc's interruption gave Kay a chance to clear her head. "I'm sorry, Leah, I didn't mean to blow up at you, but you'll just have to trust me. Improvisation is how I always start my pieces—ballet or modern—and if you want to work with me, you'll just have to try to understand."

Leah hesitated before replying. She knew Kay was talented, but trying to move as if she had never studied dance and running around in circles seemed silly to Leah—and an outright waste of time. For a moment she considered not working with Kay. Perhaps she should have listened to Finola; if she hadn't taken on this extra part she'd have been able to wrangle more time with Patrick to practice what was really important: *Dance Indigo*. Leah traced a circle with her big toe on the floor and was about to tell Kay she'd changed her mind and wouldn't work with her after all when Kay shouted, "That's it, Leah, that's it!"

"She doesn't even know what you're talking about." Linda giggled, then grabbed Leah's arm and pointed at her foot. "You were making circles with your toe. You weren't 'dancing,' you were doing a natural movement. Start from there, Leah."

Leah stared down at her feet. "Making circles with my toe," she repeated in a flat voice.

She looked up into the ring of smiling, encouraging faces. "Okay. I think I get it now," she said slowly.

Kay looked as if she had had a brainstorm. "You know, the only thing that's wrong with you, Stephenson, is that you haven't seen enough modern dance, let alone tried to dance it."

"I've seen the Graham company and Paul Taylor and—"

"Not modern enough," Kay interjected. "Not the kind of thing we're trying to do." While she talked, someone went back to the tape recorder and turned it on. The other dancers started circling again, and Kay drew Leah aside. "I know you're busy, but I've got an extra ticket and no one else wants to go with me," Kay said with a sigh.

"To what?" Leah hurled an impatient glance at

the clock. There were classes after this, then rehearsal with Finola, then she would finally get to bed.... But she couldn't let herself think that far ahead.

"There's this choreography demonstration and workshop on the Sunday before the gala. A really great choreographer from New York is in town. It'll be something you don't just listen to but get to dance and work in. I think you should come with me. I think you'd like it and—"

"Before the gala ... right before?" Leah asked. "No, Kay, I can't. I have that big performance the day after Madame's party. I just won't have time." Leah didn't add that even if she did have the time, she'd choose someplace else to go. Contemporary dance just didn't thrill her.

Kay looked at Leah hard, then shrugged. "Of course, dancing with the company has to come first. I understand, Leah."

"The timing ..." Leah tried to soften her rejection of Kay's offer.

"Stinks!" Kay argued.

Leah went back to tracing circles on the floor. It felt pretty stupid, and she didn't feel that she was dancing. But dancing or not, it certainly felt better than fighting with Kay. With Alex gone, Kay was truly Leah's best friend at SFBA.

Chapter 7

When Patrick burst through the door of the Blue Studio at six-fifteen that night, Leah and Finola were still rehearsing the newly named *Sick Chicken*.

"Patrick!" both girls shrieked, and Finola tried to hide Leah.

"What are you doing here?" the English girl said coldly. "You're staff!"

Patrick looked from Finola to Leah and slowly took in the situation. "Madame's birthday?" A smile played on his lips as he spied the ratty feather duster dangling from Leah's elastic belt. "Are you girls trying to clean up your act?"

Leah was exhausted, but she mustered up the strength to mug a face at his bad joke. "You think you're funny, don't you? But preparing for this gala is work, Patrick. Hard work!" She flopped down onto the floor and played dead.

Patrick laughed, but Finola still tried to push him toward the door. "Can't you read the sign? It says Do Not Disturb right there." She pointed to the door handle. Finola herself was struggling not to laugh. But it was important to keep the program a secret from everyone on the staff; that was part of the fun and a tradition of the gala.

"Mum's the word," Patrick said, then seemed to remember his errand. "Besides, this is in the nature of an emergency."

Leah stood up, suddenly worried. "Has something happened?"

Finola quickly removed the feather duster and stuffed it into a large canvas carryall.

"No ... but Madame wants you!"

"Now?" Leah's knees threatened to give out beneath her. "Oh, Patrick, I can't rehearse now. I'm so tired." Then she realized what she was saying. Leah took a deep breath and tugged down the back of her leotard. "Though, of course, rehearsals for *Dance Indigo* take precedence over everything else." Wearing a martyred expression, she started toward her dance bag.

Patrick's laugh stopped her. "Rehearsals? Tonight?" His tone implied that even Madame Preston wouldn't work someone that hard. "Nothing like that, Leah, but you have been summoned—"

"To what?" Finola said, eyeing Leah with sympathy. "Poor Leah, she's been dancing nonstop since this morning. She didn't even have lunch."

"To the Opera House. Madame wants you there, in the company box, to see Ashley dance Juliet."

"A performance—watch a performance in the company box?" Leah could barely get the words out. "What'll I wear?" she wailed, and bounded across the floor with renewed energy. "I haven't got a thing, and curtain's at eight, isn't it, and—"

"Does she have to go?" Finola asked, not sharing Leah's excitement at all. "Is it that important? And who in the world is this Ashley person? I know she's in the company, but where's she from?"

"She's the other girl in *Dance Indigo.* Your planes probably crossed over the Atlantic last fall when you came here from London as an exchange student. She's been guesting with the Royal Ballet since then," Patrick told them.

"So *that's* where she's been!" Leah murmured.

"And last year she spent most of her time with Nureyev's company in Paris. Her contract with Bay Area was supposed to start this fall, but the company directors felt all this international experience would give her good press, so they let her go until her performances in London were finished. See you two later! Have fun tonight," Patrick said.

"I think it's crazy going out tonight, Leah," Finola said under her breath when Patrick left the room. The school was empty for the evening, and the girls changed their clothes right in the studio. "In your shoes I'd try to beg out of it and go home to a hot meal and a bath!"

Leah looked up from slipping on her jeans. "Beg out of sitting in a box with Madame?" Leah was incredulous. "Finola Darling, in my shoes you'd do just what I'm doing.... Besides, aren't you the least bit curious? I mean, why does she want me there—on such short notice—for tonight's performance?"

"I wonder about that myself," Finola said, slipping into her miniskirt. "But don't push yourself so much, Leah. Whatever else Madame may want for you, she doesn't want you to wear yourself out. You've worked too hard today."

Leah tossed off Finola's concern with a laugh. "I'll be fine, Finola. I'm strong, and I think watching my favorite ballet from such a special spot ..." Leah stopped and gave herself a delighted little shake. "An Opera House box! I think that will revive me faster and better than a hot bath, and it certainly won't be as fattening as dinner at Mrs. Hanson's!"

An hour and ten minutes later, Leah was wearing her blue drop-waist dress, the silky one she'd bought for a party at a benefactor's house last fall. She had brushed her hair to a golden sheen, and two blue clips held the thick waves back from her face.

Leah had never sat in the company box before. The Opera House was ablaze with lights, and Madame had pushed Leah right to the front seat, next to Claire DuParc.

"Now, I want both you girls to watch this performance carefully," Madame said, as the concertmaster stood in the orchestra pit, brandished his bow in the air, and immediately stopped the random tuning of instruments. He drew his bow slowly down the A-string, and one by one the string section, the winds, the harp, and the rest of the orchestra joined in. "Especially you, Leah." Madame pulled a small, antique pair of ivory opera glasses out of her tiny, sequined evening bag and pressed them into Leah's hand. "Claire, of course, has danced Juliet many times before, though she is not familiar yet with our particular staging."

Leah just nodded. She wasn't sure how to respond. Then Madame stepped out of the box, and Leah heard Andrei Levintoff's distinctive Russian accent out in the corridor. She waited for Madame to answer him, and only then did she dare to ask Claire, "What's going on?" She fiddled nervously with the hem of her dress.

Claire turned to Leah. "You don't know?" when Leah shook her head, Claire bit her lip. "Andrei didn't say *anything*?"

Leah drew in her breath. She barely knew Claire. The young ballerina was guesting with the Bay Area Ballet this season and had only arrived in town about a month ago. She was Andrei's fiancée, and Leah longed to know her better. But so far their schedules had kept them from exchanging more than a few words.

Claire started to speak, then quickly put a finger to her lips. Madame had returned to the box, followed by Andrei.

"Leah, you are here!" He kissed Claire first, then dropped down in the seat just behind Leah and lightly touched her hair. "I am so glad you are to be in *Dance Indigo*. You are so different from Ashley when you dance. It shall be a perfect pairing, I think. Madame is pleased with your dance, too." Then he actually winked at Madame Preston.

Only Andrei, Leah thought, could do that and make Madame smile.

"Yes, Leah shows great promise these days," Madame said graciously, and the two patrons seated in the back of the box regarded Leah with interest. She met their frank gazes with a shy smile, then turned around, keeping her back very straight. As the houselights went down, she felt a blush creep up her neck.

As the conductor came to the podium, the audience burst into applause, then stopped just as quickly as he raised his baton. There was a moment of silence, then the opening chords of the Prokofiev score resonated through the great and gilded auditorium. Leah felt the barest touch of a cool hand on her back. She turned her head slightly. It was Madame. She leaned her silver head toward Leah and whispered, "You watch, Leah, watch Ashley. She is a wonderful Juliet and I think you can learn a lot from her performance. This will be of great help to you when your turn comes to dance this."

Leah's eyes widened with disbelief. The curtain lifted, and this time the thrill she felt to see the gorgeous Italian Renaissance set was even greater than usual. What had Madame been hinting at? Was she about to cast Leah as Juliet? Leah tried to remind herself that that just didn't make sense; so many girls in the Bay Area company were studying the part. Claire herself had first billing, and now Ashley, and after a few weeks of filming Diana would be back in the lineup, and she was the favorite local star. Still, Madame had brought her here tonight for a reason. Leah would ask Claire the minute she got her alone about Madame's plans.

Unfortunately, it wasn't until the final curtain that Leah and Claire had a chance to talk. "Wasn't that incredible?' the auburn-haired woman cried. "I haven't seen Ashley Phillips dance in absolutely years, and she's grown so ..." Claire shrugged her tiny shoulders. "I don't know the word for it."

Leah didn't know, either, except that she suddenly felt quite privileged to be slotted to share the matinee with a ballerina of Ashley's caliber. But even Ashley's inspired interpretation of the Shakespearean heroine hadn't taken Leah's mind off her future.

"Claire," she said in a soft voice as they filed out of the box and into the corridor. "What was Andrei supposed to tell me?" Leah's voice trembled slightly. "I mean, about some kind of plan of Madame's."

Claire's eyes softened with pity. "You poor kid, I sort of left all that hanging, didn't I." She tucked Leah's hand through her arm and guided her down the side hall where the crowd was thinner. As they slowly strolled down the passageway, she said, "Well, it wasn't about you, really." Seeing the dismay on Leah's face, she hurried to explain. "Not at first. You see, Madame wanted to cast Andrei's friend, the girl from Leningrad, as Juliet next month with the touring group."

"Andrei's friend from Leningrad? You mean Madame had that kind of plan for Alex and didn't *tell* her?" Leah had to fight back the angry comment rising to her lips. She knew Claire wasn't responsible for this terrible mistake. "Claire," she finally said, "if Alex had known, she wouldn't have left school."

"No, Leah. Alex *did* know. Andrei told her the night of her party. She could have changed her mind."

"Alex never mentioned this. She would have

told me, I'm sure...." Leah's voice trailed off. Would Alex have confided in her? she wondered. Maybe they had grown further apart than she'd thought.

"Hey, it's not such a big deal. Lots of gifted girls quit dancing."

But Alex was more than just a gifted girl. Didn't Claire realize that? Leah looked down at the carpet. Thousands of feet had worn down the once-deep pile, as ballet and opera lovers filed through the Opera House night after night to see great performers. Alex would have been one of the really great ones, Leah was sure of it. And suddenly Leah knew in her heart that Claire had just told her the truth. Alex had quit dancing in spite of the promise of starring as Juliet.

Leah could feel Claire's eyes watching her. "Sorry about that—yes, Alex probably did know. She just didn't tell me."

"Men!" Claire suddenly exclaimed, seeming to change the topic. "They never know what is important."

Claire responded to Leah's baffled look with a laugh. "Andrei should have told you that. I mean, you are friends. But I think with this dumb movie, he would forget his feet if they weren't attached to him."

As they passed the hall mirror, Claire stopped to tighten the belt on her short black wool dress. A black velvet ribbon had been worked into her French braid, and Leah couldn't help but stare at the lovely diamond she wore on her left hand. Andrei certainly had nice taste in engagement rings. And in women, Leah found herself thinking.

"Thanks, Claire, for sharing all this," she said, a little shy about expressing her feelings to someone she really didn't know that well.

"For sharing what?" Claire smiled. "But I haven't gotten to the good part...." Her brown eyes sparkled. "Or maybe you've guessed?"

"The good part," Leah said slowly, then her hands flew to her face. Her blue eyes stared at Claire over the tips of her fingers. "You don't mean ..." Leah's voice was muffled by her palms.

Claire looked around, then whispered, "Yes, they're thinking of you."

"Me?" Leah's voice squeaked very loudly and Claire winced. Leah grabbed her hand. "You mean they—they might let me dance Juliet with the company?"

"With the tour group on the spring trip," Claire was careful to point out. "I guess Madame is waiting to break the big news until after the premiere of *Dance Indigo*. Too much for the nerves, all these breaks," Claire said lightly, then surprised Leah by kissing her on the cheek. "But good luck to you. From what I've seen of your dancing, you're ready for a chance like this."

Leah leaned against the wall. She heard familiar voices coming from around the corner, and Claire motioned for her to head back into the main corridor, where people were already gathering to go down to the lobby for a postperformance party. Leah shook her head. "I'll be down in a minute," she said. She looked around and pointed to the ladies' room.

Claire blew her a kiss, then breezed off toward the stairwell. Leah didn't bother to duck inside the bathroom. No one was around now. She tip-toed back to the empty box, leaned against the railing, and stared dreamily at the stage. Already the stagehands were breaking down the set. Two burly men were dismantling Juliet's tomb, and the hard foam-rubber surface where Ashley had lain only minutes before bounced as one of the crew hoisted it above his head and made for the wings. Ushers with brooms and carpet sweepers were cleaning the aisles. Music wafted up the stairs from the lobby. The party had already started.

The houselights were on, and under the glare the empty auditorium looked rather shabby: the gilt was peeling off the carved trim of the proscenium, and from her vantage point, Leah noticed that the floorboards on the stage needed polishing. All the light and magic of the performance had vanished. But Leah didn't care. She allowed her mind to drift and pictured herself in Ashley's last-act costume, the pale negligée she'd worn when Juliet had poisoned herself. Leah sighed and, turning around, hugged her arms to her chest.

Leaning back against the railing, she stared into the back of the box and through the open door to the brightly lit hall beyond. So much was happening so fast. First *Dance Indigo,* now this. She might actually dance a full-length ballet with the company before she turned sixteen. How would she ever thank Madame?

The answer popped instantly into Leah's mind: By dancing the best she could.

Chapter 8

Down in the Opera House lobby the caterers had been busy. Buffet tables lined the walls and the bar buzzed with conversation. Glasses tinkled amid the laughter of the hundred or so dancers, corporate and private benefactors, and *Temptations* personnel invited to the postperformance party. The film crew looked as uncomfortable in their jeans and pink-lettered *Temptations* T-shirts and jackets as Leah felt.

The buffet had only just begun and already Leah's smile felt as stiff as starch. Kay had once said that part of the curriculum at any well-respected dance academy should be the how-to-shake-hands-and-smile-and-say-nice-things-to-benefactors course. Leah found herself shunted between one group of patrons and another—first by Madame, and then by Andrei, who had temporarily left her with Ashley. Big mistake, Leah thought. The bubbly strawberry blonde was so busy signing autographs that when some people couldn't get next to her, they settled for Leah.

"So you're the bright new star," a businessman

said, and his diamond-bedecked wife practically fell over Leah. Leah had the distinct impression that they were somehow getting her mixed up with Ashley. No one had introduced Leah to them, and they probably thought she had been the evening's Juliet. "We're the Austins," the woman announced, and glowed at Leah. "You must come visit us next time you're in Marin."

"Why, thank you!" Leah replied. At one of her first company functions Leah had made the mistake of trying to explain that dancers, particularly SFBA students, never had time off and never "just happened to be" anywhere but at rehearsal!

Leah had since learned that the hard work and intense dedication that marked a dancer's life seldom interested most of their audience. It was the illusion of dance—the ease of movement, the incredible grace—that mattered, even to the most devoted fans. No one wanted to hear about the long hours, terrible rehearsal schedules, aching muscles, and oceans of sweat.

The crowd surged forward, then back again, and all at once Leah found herself on the outskirts. She heaved a relieved sigh and looked around for someone she knew. Andrei and Claire had vanished into the throng of fans. Company members smiled at Leah from across the room, then went back to their conversations. Leah was suddenly aware that outside of Andrei, and to some degree Patrick, she really wasn't friends with anyone in the company, at least not yet. If only Kay and the rest of her friends were here!

Leah leaned back against the wall and put her plastic goblet of seltzer down in a convenient niche. She closed her eyes for a minute and wondered if she should have taken Finola's advice and stayed home after all. It was already eleven P.M., and every muscle in her body was sore.

A tap on her shoulder made her jump.

She whirled around and looked up. A tall, striking girl was smiling down at her. Leah blinked. The girl looked so familiar. Her chin-length hair was thick and black and curled under slightly. Below her severe and straight bangs were a pair of huge, almond-shaped dark eyes.

"Alex?" Leah croaked in disbelief. "Alexandra Sorokin!" With every syllable her voice grew louder. She was so excited she bounced a little on her toes. "What are you doing here?"

Several people turned around at the sound of Leah's voice but Alex was too quick for them. She pulled Leah behind a statue and said, "I am gone only two and a half weeks—"

"Three," Leah corrected instantly.

"Three then." Alex shrugged carelessly. "And you do not recognize me." Her full red lips parted in a smile. "Though you look different, too."

Leah's heart was filled with a confusion of emotions. She wanted to scream and shout for joy, but Alex hadn't called, not once. She hadn't dropped a note. She could have plummeted off the face of the earth for all Leah knew. And remembering what Claire had just told her about Alex being picked for Juliet, she wanted to walk away, turn her back on Alex, and never speak to her again.

"We have to talk!" Alex said. With her usual verve, Alex snagged a small serving plate of caviar and crackers. Leaving Leah to grab something to drink, she headed confidently for the back steps, the ones that led backstage and to the garage.

"Stop, Alex! Stop right now." Leah had followed meekly for all of two seconds. "I can't just walk out of here. Madame would—"

"What Madame does not know will not hurt her," Alex reminded her in her thick Russian accent. "And besides, we do not leave here, we simply leave all the noise."

Alex dropped down onto a heavily carpeted step and patted the floor next to her. "Come now, we have to talk. I do not have so very much time. I must get back soon. I have a ride back to Berkeley with a very cute guy from the film crew." Alex's eyes sparkled with anticipation.

"Cute guy?" Leah repeated, staring at Alex. There was so much to say, so many questions to ask, that Leah didn't know where to start. "Alex, what did you *do* to yourself?" she asked suddenly, unable to stop herself.

Hurt flickered in Alex's eyes.

"Don't get me wrong—I like how you look! You look fantastic, great, dynamite!" With each adjective Alex brightened more.

"But you cut your hair," Leah wailed. "And your dress—it's red!" The whole time she'd known Alex, the Russian girl had dressed in black and white. Now she looked like a completely different person, one Leah didn't know.

Alex seemed to be enjoying the effect she was having on Leah. She daintily bit into a wheat cracker and chewed it well before replying. "I change my life, so I think it is time to change my picture—"

"Your image!" Leah corrected Alex out of habit. Then both girls stared at each other and at exactly the same instant started laughing.

As soon as they recovered, they declared in unison. "I miss you!" Then they collapsed in laughter all over again.

"But I really do!" Alex declared finally, still smiling.

"I'm only a phone call away!" Leah reminded her.

"Touché! Stephenson, I know I do not call, but how can I say it? I am so busy and there are so many new things. It is still hard, you know—I have danced all my life."

For a moment Alex's guard dropped and Leah got a glimpse of how difficult it had been for her to leave SFBA on the brink of a real dance career. A heartbeat later, Leah thought she had been imagining things. Alex was again attacking her caviar with gusto and saying, "But I think I made the right decision. And to call you at the boardinghouse as if nothing had changed ... it would be too difficult. I had to be alone for a while. To make a new beginning, not hold on to an end."

"But everyone was worried about you, Alex."

"I know. Andrei told me so when he picked me up."

"That's how you got here!" Leah's unasked question had been answered. Now that she thought of it, Claire had arrived at the Opera House on time and alone. Andrei had made that last-minute entrance into the box with Madame.

"Yes, he said that everyone is unhappy not to see me and he was able to scrounge a ticket for tonight. This Ashley Phillips is a beautiful dancer, no!" Alex sighed and drew a strand of her hair under her nose and twirled it absently like a mustache. Leah had never seen her do anything so silly before. "But I wish Kay were here, too, and Katrina and Finola and Linda."

Leah nodded. "The party was such a drag until you turned up." She almost told Alex that if she missed her friends so much, she should drop by once in a while. After all, she knew where they all lived.

Alex studied Leah for a moment, then asked, "So how come you were honored tonight? Getting comps to a benefit performance when everything is so expensive is not usual. Andrei mumbled something about seeing you in Madame's box."

"He didn't tell you?"

"He tells me you miss me and says he wants me to be a big surprise. That's all." Alex squinted her large brown eyes and studied Leah. "Something, I think, has happened to you—you are different. And you have not changed your hair, and I know this dress. You look . . ." Leah was about to suggest a word to Alex, but Alex put up her hand to stop her. She wanted to find the right word herself. "Radiant . . ." She tested it, then grinned. "That means you glow!"

Leah blushed a little deeper. She grinned back at Alex.

Alex narrowed her eyes and said in a superior voice, "I told you Peter was not such a bad thing. Tell me, Leah, when did you decide to see him again?"

"Pe-Peter?" Leah sputtered and almost spilled her seltzer on her dress. "Believe me, the changes that are happening in my life have nothing to do with Peter! Nothing's going on in the romance department."

Alex's face fell. "So, then what has happened? You do look different." This time Alex eyed Leah more critically.

Leah hesitated. It hurt knowing that Alex, her most trusted confidante at the school up until a few weeks ago, would be twice as interested in Leah's love life—if she had one—than in the news that she was about to become a real star.

"I got a part," she began.

"So what else is new?" Alex paused to sip her juice. "You always get all the big parts—especially without me around to compete with." She let out a throaty, good-natured laugh.

Leah bopped Alex on the head with her program, then grinned.

"Alexandra, this is *not* your basic, run-of-the-mill, everyday part." Leah smiled and let the suspense grow. "I am going to dance with the company, Alex—with Patrick and Ashley—in that ballet of Madame's. You know, *Dance Indigo*. The one scheduled to be revived for Diana. Only she couldn't do it, so I am."

Alex was stunned. "With the company? Madame is letting you dance a lead with the company?" Disbelief shadowed Alex's high-cheekboned face. "After she told you you were too young for a career!" She sounded disgusted.

Leah tried to digest the fact that Alex was actually criticizing Madame Preston. Alex, who had stuck up for the stern Academy director through thick and thin and who had agreed that Leah shouldn't take the lead in *Temptations,* no matter what.

In light of Madame's other plans for her, Leah felt obliged to come to the director's defense. "A movie is different from dancing on the stage, even you said that. I think I am mature enough, and good enough, to perform a one-act piece with the company."

"Yes, I know that. But so soon . . ." Alex foundered. Then she colored slightly. "You know, I am still jealous. Would you believe it? But I think Madame was right. This is a good thing for you and for the school. Madame should let her best students perform in public, show them off now and then," Alex concluded with great firmness.

"Well, she certainly tried to show you off, what with offering you Juliet—"

Alex paled. "Who told you this?"

Leah debated with herself for only an instant before replying, "Andrei told Claire. Tonight it sort of came up." For some reason, Leah held back from mentioning the possibility of Madame giving her the role in the near future.

Alex studied her hands. "I found out the night I was leaving."

"It wasn't too late, you could have changed your mind," Leah argued. "Unless it was a matter of the Sorokin pride."

Alex waved her off with a gesture. "Pride? No. I made my decision, and like I told you, it was not just because of the auditions for companies that did not work. Maybe if I had gotten into Joffrey or

ABT, or even here, I would have lasted a year or two longer. But I would have stopped dancing, anyway." Alex let out a long sigh. "Not even performing Juliet could tempt me. Leah, do not tell everyone about this. Madame would be upset. She does not plan for other girls to have that part—too many company members are fighting over it."

Leah caught her breath, but silently agreed to Alex's request.

"And what has happened to my room?" Alex asked in a slightly wistful tone.

"You're not going to believe it."

"Not Pam!" Alex bellowed.

"Nope."

"You?" Alex brightened. "I had hoped Mrs. Hanson would give it to you. In fact, I told her so before I left, but she was very mysterious."

"No, not me." Leah purposely delayed responding, trying to build the suspense. "Sophie got it."

"Who is Sophie?"

"She's new, and—get a load of this—she is a prodigy."

Alex looked skeptical.

"She's twelve, and Madame has admitted her to the school. She'll be taking academic classes at the junior high down the block from the Academy. Otherwise she studies right along with us."

"Madame did this?" Alex looked very worried. "Someone must have forced her. She does not believe in prodigies. She thinks being singled out like that ruins dancers. The name, Sophie—Sophie what?"

"Potter!"

"Ah!" Alex recognized it instantly. "The girl with the prize." She sighed. "I wish I could meet her someday. I wonder how my friends are back at the Vaganova Institute. I hear this girl, she studied there. I wonder if she knows anyone I know."

"Well, I'm sure Madame had her reasons for letting Sophie come here," Leah maintained.

Alex's face darkened. "No, I think someone in the company ... the directors, they make pressure for her. They tell her what to do, because a girl like that is a box-office hit." Alex pondered something for a moment, then said with great conviction. "I predict Madame will have to offer *her* the Juliet."

"Oh, no!" Leah gasped before she could stop herself. Pam's prediction was already coming true: Sophie would soon be in direct competition with her.

Alex was quick to catch Leah's reaction. "Has Madame offered the part with the touring group to you?"

Fortunately, Leah could be perfectly honest with Alex and not reveal her secret. "No. Madame hasn't done anything like that." She thought she had better change the subject before the discussion went any further. "I can't believe you left when you did, Alexandra Sorokin!" She forced herself to sound playful. There was no point worrying about Juliet; Madame hadn't offered it to her yet, and there was still *Dance Indigo* to get through. Leah could deal with her feelings about Sophie later.

"Why?" Alex answered.

"You abandoned ship before the birthday gala! Finola's doing a great job, but she doesn't know

the ropes in the school like you do." Leah proceeded to fill Alex in one the plans for the performance. Alex laughed a lot at first, until Leah
started describing her rehearsal that afternoon
with Kay.

"You must be crazy, Stephenson," she said.

"Why?"

"Taking on so much. With the big company
performance, I think I wouldn't even be in the
gala, except for something very small—like *The
Dying Pigeon.*"

"*The Sick Chicken!*" Leah corrected her with a
giggle.

Alex shrugged and wrapped a lacy black shawl
around her bare shoulders. The stairwell was getting cold, and from the faint sound of foghorns in
the Bay, the girls could tell a mist was rising. "That
sounds easy. You know the steps to *The Dying
Swan.* You just have to make them funny, no?"

"More or less." Leah shrugged.

"But with the big performance the next day...
Leah, you shouldn't take such a chance to be in
two pieces the night before. And Kay's dancing—it
is so, so wrong for you. For your body. You are
not a modern dancer, and you must be at your
very best for your debut."

Leah laughed uncomfortably. "It's not such a
big deal, really."

"You are stretching yourself too thin. Why do
you do this? You used to seem sensible—that is
what it is about you that is different." Alex sounded
upset. She stared at Leah. "Something in your
face—it makes you look like James."

"James Cummings?" Leah asked. "With black

hair and brown eyes and ..." She attempted to lower her voice, to sound like her former, rather sexy partner.

"Do not make a joke with me about this!" Alex said adamantly. "You look as if you are too hungry to be a star, you want to rush things. You must not work so hard. Do the best you can for Madame's ballet and forget about this silly birthday thing."

"Really, Alex, I know the limits of my own body!" Leah snapped, suddenly peeved.

"I think not. You are acting like James, and you know how he got hurt that time and almost hurt you when he would not listen," Alex argued.

Leah was horrified at Alex's suggestion. Earlier that year James had been Leah's partner in a dance demonstration at a local high school. While they were rehearsing for a pas de deux from *Romeo and Juliet,* James had injured himself. But instead of being sensible and resting, he had pushed himself—and Leah—even harder. A few days later disaster followed during their performance when James fell and ended up on crutches.

"This is not the same kind of situation, not at all," Leah contended. "I am not pushing myself as hard as James pushed himself—and me—last fall. I'm not, Alex, and besides"—Leah stood up, "I don't think it's your place to discuss my dancing."

Alex frowned. "What do you mean?"

"You are not a dancer anymore. You quit, Alex. And you have no right to judge me. Madame chose me to dance with the company—and I'm only in my first year here. If she believes in me, that's all that matters. I don't need permission from you."

Leah turned on her heel and started to walk back toward the lobby.

"Stephenson, do not do this!" Alex yelled after her. She tossed the plastic serving plate into a trash can near the water fountain and jogged up in front of Leah, blocking her way. "Let us not make a fight." A knowing smile played at the corners of Alex's lips. "I will not say I am sorry"—she put her hand up to keep Leah from interrupting—"because I know I am right. But maybe you are right, too. You have to make your own decisions—like I did about leaving school. Sometimes there are mistakes and sometimes you do the right thing. But we are friends and that is no mistake. As long as I can tell you what I think without you being so—so—"

Leah dropped her eyes. "So defensive," she admitted softly. "But I do know what I'm doing. Trust me."

There was an awkward silence, then the girls started back to the lobby, arm in arm. "Tell me, how's Ben?" Leah asked, steering toward a safer topic.

Alex shrugged. "Okay, I guess. I see him now and then."

"But, Alex, you were in love with Ben!" Leah was shocked. The Alex she had known was loyal, true-blue, unswerving. Kay and Leah had planned to go to Ben and Alex's wedding someday.

"I am in love with many people now—or maybe many people are in love with me!" she said with great satisfaction. "There is Joshua and Daniel and Richard and—"

Leah clapped her hands over her ears. "I don't

need a list of boyfriends, please." But she had to laugh. Alex looked so happy—and beautiful. Who could blame all those college men for falling in love with her?

"But speaking of love!" Alex grabbed Leah's arm and squeezed it until it hurt. "Look," she whispered, tugging Leah behind a potted plant.

Leah did a double-take. "I don't believe it!" In the lobby, Diana Chang and James were standing with their arms wrapped around each other's waists. "James and Diana! Is he nuts?"

"No, ambitious!" Alex said sourly. "With no taste in women!"

"I don't think we should be looking," Leah said, and turned away as James nuzzled Diana's ear.

"I don't *want* to look!" Alex laughed.

They stole into what was left of the thinning crowd. But Leah had to have one last word. "Please take it back, Alex," she pleaded.

"Take what back?" Alex had retrieved her coat from the checkroom and was waving at the boy who'd promised to give her a ride back to Berkeley.

"What you said about James—I'm not like him. Not at all."

Alex moistened her lips, then sighed. "You are not like him *that* way—you would never date someone to get ahead. No, you are not exactly like him." And that was as much as she would budge on that point.

Chapter 9

Leah had penned her name on the sign-in sheet and was halfway up the first flight of stairs before Andrei's car had pulled away from the boardinghouse. Leah had forgotten to thank him for the ride back, but she was sure he'd understand. Even though the opera house was only ten minutes away from Mrs. Hanson's, she was so exhausted that she had actually dropped off to sleep in the backseat.

Leah yawned widely and wondered why she loved her top-floor room. Mrs. Hanson had been right. Coming home at night and having to climb all those stairs was the last straw sometimes. Leah cast a sleepy glance toward the closed door of Alex's old room. She had almost walked by when she heard a noise coming from inside.

She hesitated for a moment just outside the door. She hadn't been in the room once since Alex had left the SFBA. Leah hadn't wanted to go in there, but now, as she heard a gasp followed by a long, heartbreaking sob, she knew she had to talk to Sophie. She sounded miserable.

Leah didn't bother to knock; she pushed the door open slowly and said, "Sophie?"

Street light filtered through the flimsy curtains. The sobs were apparently coming from the bed, though all Leah could see in the shadows was a lumpy heap. Sophie's stuffed animals, Leah thought. Then she saw the longer, thinner shadow that ended under the pillows. "Sophie, what's the matter?" Leah asked quietly. She felt her way along the wall to the bed, then shoved the hill of plush figures aside so that she could sit down.

The sobbing stopped. What looked to be a wrinkle beneath the sheets wriggled, and then Sophie looked up. In the shadows her small face seemed swollen. She'd been crying for hours, Leah realized with a pang.

"What are you doing here?" Sophie asked. She sniffed back her tears and rubbed her nightgown sleeve across her nose. Leah thought to reach for the light, to find some tissues, but she didn't want to embarrass the girl.

"I just got in from a performance at the Opera House. I heard you crying—"

Sophie turned her head away.

Leah fiddled with the strap of her small shoulderbag. "I cried, too, when I first got here. Are you homesick?" She didn't add that she hadn't expected Sophie to be homesick—Sophie had spent a year halfway across the world!

"Yes, I guess I'm that . . ." Sophie sniffed and then sat up again. Her face was pale in the dark. "Homesick."

Leah, who hated people to see her face when

she cried, was surprised when Sophie flicked on the bedside lamp. Sophie's hair was wild and tangled, and Leah wondered how she'd ever get the knots out in the morning. On impulse, Leah looked around the room, hoping to spot a brush.

Alex's room—Alex's wonderful, homey room— was a mess. Not that Leah had expected Sophie or her mom to get her stuff together so soon. But even without the heaps of clothes and open suitcases, Leah could see Sophie's room was never going to be very neat—or pretty. The curtains were off-white and the rocking chair Alex had left behind looked bare without its heap of colorful pillows. The bookshelves were empty, except for a dual-sided tapedeck-radio with cartoon stickers pasted all over it. Leah decided to make a project of tackling Sophie's room, helping her make herself comfortable here.

A sturdy, plastic-handled brush poked out from beneath a pile of leotards. Leah reached over to the cluttered dresser, grabbed it, and gently turned Sophie around so that she could brush her hair. Sophie drew her knees up under the covers and seemed to relax as Leah gently tried to work out the tangles.

A few minutes passed in companionable silence. As Leah brushed and brushed the thick brown waves, she tried to remember what it was like to be twelve. It felt like ages since she and Chrissy had set off for the seventh grade at San Lorenzo Junior High. Even though she was only three years older, Leah couldn't imagine being twelve and already talked about as a major star in newspapers and magazines.

When Sophie finally spoke, it was as if she had read Leah's mind. "It's not just being homesick," she said in her startlingly deep voice. She suddenly turned around and faced Leah. She took the brush from her hand and began yanking it through her hair herself. After a few tugs, so brusque they made Leah wince in sympathy, Sophie let the brush fall to her lap. "It's having no friends—ever. It's all the jealousy. None of the girls here are ever going to give me a chance."

"What makes you say that?" Leah was astounded. What could have happened to make Sophie jump to such a conclusion? She hadn't even been over to the school yet—at least not to classes.

Sophie bit her lip, then raised her huge, deep eyes and looked plaintively at Leah. "I've been through it before. It was awful in Leningrad, and before that it was awful back in Florida—that's where I'm from originally. No one liked me there, either. I pretend I don't care, but—"

"It won't be like that here!" Leah interrupted adamantly. "It won't. SFBA is very competitive—we all compete with each other, we get jealous, but most of us stay friends, when all is said and done."

Sophie didn't look convinced. "That's not the impression I had tonight. People are jealous of *you*," she said shyly. "I don't blame them. You look like a beautiful dancer."

Leah blushed at the compliment, but she couldn't let Sophie's remark go by. "What people? Do you mean here in the boardinghouse?"

Sophie nodded.

"Pam's always that way. We've had problems since we got here last September. But she's not typical of the other girls."

"It wasn't Pam, Leah. It was the other ones: Kay, her roommate Linda, Suzanne, and then two girls who don't live here—Fiona—the one with the English accent."

"Finola," Leah corrected. "She was here, tonight?"

"With Katrina—I like her. But they were all talking about you." Sophie hesitated, then swept her hair away from her face. "I shouldn't gossip, but I thought they were your friends."

Leah had thought so, too. She took a deep breath. "What did they say, Sophie?" Even as she asked, she wondered if she was doing the right thing.

"That Madame picked you for some special ballet and how it wasn't fair."

"Oh, but Kay practically said that to my face the other day," Leah said.

Sophie seemed surprised. "Kay said you were acting—I don't remember the exact words—stuck up, something like that. And Finola said you were going through a hard time and it was tough working with you. Katrina said she didn't blame you and—"

Leah put her hands to her ears. She didn't want to hear any more. "I get the point! They were jealous," she added. Jealousy was to be expected. Then why did she feel so surprised and hurt to know that her closest friends were talking about her behind her back?

"But I felt that if they talked that way about

you, they must talk that way about me, too. After all, I'm new, and I'm not even anyone's friend—yet." She stopped and just looked at Leah, her eyes bright with hope.

"You're my friend, Sophie," Leah told her. "And I promise I'll be yours."

"And I'll never be jealous of you, I promise," Sophie added.

Leah looked up quickly. "No, I'm sure you won't." To herself, she added, Why should you be? Then she got up and said good night. Just as she reached the door, she turned around.

"Sophie, about all this gossip ... It's normal around here. I don't think anyone was being ... well, unfriendly to me." The words seemed to come to Leah as an inspiration. She had never quite thought of this before. "I think in Kay's or Katrina's or any other girl's shoes, I'd be a little upset with me, too. You see, Madame has given me a break, the kind of thing that every dancer dreams of. Someday she'll do that for you, too."

Sophie turned out the light as Leah shut the door behind her and headed upstairs. But halfway up to her room she sat down on the steps and began to cry. She wasn't sure exactly why. What she had said to Sophie was true: Kay and everyone else had a right to be jealous of her. But it still hurt—and Kay was wrong: Leah wasn't stuck-up. Alex had hinted at the problem tonight; clearly, Madame had stopped holding Leah back. And now that she was beginning to live the life of a real dancer, she felt as if she had outgrown the school in some ways. Finola and everyone else had to be sensing that she'd outgrown them a bit, too, in the past few days. Her heart just wasn't in the gala, even though she was participating in it. It was their pet project, and she was rejecting it as silly and childish. No wonder they were upset!

She'd show them that she could do both: be a professional *and* a friend.

Chapter 10

"So what's the big secret?" *Kay's voice* so startled Leah that she almost spilled her soup as she sat down at their regular table in the cafeteria the next day at noon.

She knows about Juliet! was Leah's first thought.

Suzanne looked up from sipping her milk and mumbled, "Yeah, you've been awfully quiet today. You are the one girl here who got to see Ashley Phillips's performance. The critic in the *Examiner* said it was the best Juliet he'd ever seen."

"There's no secret," Leah said, relieved. "And how can you say I haven't told you anything when I haven't even been around?"

"You can say that again," Katrina complained. "This morning we were supposed to meet down in the wardrobe room to sort out gala costumes. You—"

"And half a dozen other people I could name but won't," Finola interjected.

"You weren't there."

"This is the first time I've heard about any wardrobe session," Leah said in self-defense.

"But I left a note for you last night before Katrina and I went home, on Mrs. Hanson's sign-in sheet," Finola said.

Leah stretched and rubbed her eyes."Oh, I guess I didn't see it. I got in so late from the benefit party after the performance."

"But you weren't in your room this morning when I left!" Abigail pointed out.

"I had something to do before class." Leah didn't want to discuss her slight transgression of school rules. Ever since James's accident, Madame had forbidden students to work without a staff member present in Academy studios. This morning Leah had been in one of the forbidden third-floor practice rooms getting ready for this afternoon's rehearsal with Madame. She had barely made it down the back stairs before the *Temptations* crew arrived. She had also been two minutes late for her morning class.

Finola laughed. "Well, we can't do anything else about wardrobe until Sunday. Mrs. Slavinska has donated a trunkful of old costumes for the gala. I got the spare key from her this morning, but she said we can't rummage through the stuff until then. Too many company fittings going on." Finola sighed, then took a closer look at Leah. "But I'd say that what you needed to do this morning was sleep!"

"Now you sound like Alex!"

"*Alex!*" five voices shouted at once.

"When did you talk to Alex?" Kay was obviously peeved that Leah hadn't told her about this development first.

Leah rolled her eyes. "Last night. She was at the ballet."

"Alex actually went to the Opera House? She went to a benefit performance?" Abigail's mouth fell open, then she pursed her thin lips. "Of course, Ben Lydgate is rich and his mother has an in with management, but weren't tickets like a hundred dollars or so?"

"Don't tell me she was in Madame's box with you!" Kay was obviously flabbergasted by the idea. "None of *us* got to go!"

"It's not such a big deal, Kay!" Leah's voice trembled, and she put her spoon down hard on her tray, making it clatter. "Alex doesn't go to school anymore, so there's no reason to be jealous of her," Leah said, even though she knew she wasn't being fair. In Kay's shoes she'd be jealous, too.

"What's with you?" Linda asked Leah. "Of course Kay's jealous; we all are. Madame summoned you to some gala performance at the last minute. I think we have a right to ask why—"

"I don't *know* why," she retorted. And she hadn't at first, so that was the truth. Turning to Kay, she exclaimed, "And I didn't know Alex would be there. Andrei tracked her down in Berkeley. He was worried about her, too. I don't know how he got her into the Opera House, but he did. She didn't have a box seat, and I was pretty surprised to see her, let me tell you."

"You could have told us earlier that you'd seen her," Kay pouted, then stabbed her fork into her salad. "You don't tell me anything anymore."

"There isn't much to tell," Leah began, then let out a deep sigh. She flipped her thick French braid over her shoulder. "Oh, maybe there is; I just had so much on my mind before class today.

I would have gotten around to it later—at rehearsal or tonight."

"So, has she changed much?" Finola asked, quickly trying to break the tension in the air. "Is school working out for her?"

Leah had planned a light, quick lunch followed by another half-hour practice for *Dance Indigo* in the seldom-used ground-floor studio behind the auditorium. She didn't exactly want to spend her precious time in a gossip session. But there was no way out now—especially after hearing that her friends thought her good fortune had gone to her head and that she was a snob. Besides, everyone *had* been worried about Alex. Leah had to at least tell them that she was all right.

She glanced at her Betty Boop watch, then launched into a brief account of her conversation with Alex.

"That's it?" Kay inquired, absently zipping and unzipping her red hooded sweatshirt. "We haven't seen her for three weeks, and that's all she had to say?"

"Well, there were a couple of other things," she said, hedging. "But I don't have time to go into them now." She pushed back her chair and, picking up her dance bag in one hand and her tray in the other, started for the door. If she rushed, she'd still get in twenty minutes of work before her character class began.

The small, narrow room tucked behind the row of school offices was stuffy, and the boxes stacked against the one mirrored wall made it hard to check her positions. But Leah decided to go through with her plans to work, anyway. In her out-of-tune voice she softly hummed the main theme of her first solo, the part before Patrick's entrance. The steps themselves were easy, but the phrasing was quirky and difficult. Leah half marked, half danced her way in a series of diagonal spins and slides across the floor. The studio was so tiny that Leah could only get half the steps in before she reached the opposite wall.

"I don't believe this!" she muttered, kicking the wall in aggravation. A voice seemed to answer her.

Leah's head jerked up. She looked first in the mirror, then over her shoulder. No one was there. "I must be really tired. I'm hearing things!" she said aloud, and tried to laugh.

Then the voice said something again and she realized it was coming from the office right on the other side of the thin plasterboard wall.

"I think Leah's in some kind of trouble." Katrina's Vermont accent was easy to recognize. Leah stopped in her tracks. Sophie hadn't made that whole thing up, about the girls talking about Leah behind her back. But who was Katrina talking to, and what was on the other side of the wall?

Leah stared in dismay at the wall, then suddenly realized what was happening. Kay was in the admissions office working. Like several other students at the Academy, Kay was on a partial scholarship. She worked about six hours a week, filing cards and typing labels, but mostly gathering gossip. Today was one of Kay's non-character class days when she was scheduled to put in a two-hour work session. From the sound of the conversation coming through the wall, she was taking advantage of the Admissions secretary being out to lunch.

Kay snorted in reply. "The only trouble she's got these days in a swelled head!"

"That's not fair," Finola said. "I think we'd all find that kind of sudden change in our lives pretty upsetting."

"What in the world's upsetting about getting to dance with the company at a big premiere—even if it is just a one-act ballet?"

Leah didn't catch the beginning of Finola's reply, but the end of it made her livid. "... Leah's just in over her head. I think it has to do with Alex. I think Leah's scared to death that something will come along to make her quit dancing."

"Nothing will do that, Finola Darling. And you're wrong; for once, dead wrong!" Leah whispered to the wall. "Alex doesn't threaten me, and performing with the company isn't making me fall apart." Leah didn't want to hang around to hear the rest. She felt betrayed by her friends, but before she could gather her things, she heard Katrina's puzzled voice.

"I don't understand why Madame doesn't see all this. Shouldn't she talk to Leah? I mean, obviously *we* can't."

"You can say that again!" Kay grumbled, then dropped her voice. "I feel like the Leah Stephenson I know and love has vanished into thin air— the same black hole Alex dropped into." She sounded hurt and angry. "So talking to her is impossible, but working with her ..." Kay's voice trailed off. Then with great frustration she continued, "I don't know why she's even bothering to be in my piece. She seems bored with it. And to tell you the truth, she's not very good at my kind of choreography. She's so classical, and—I don't know—so stiff, so unyielding."

Leah cringed. How could one of her best friends be so critical of her dancing? It was good enough for Madame, wasn't it?

"Ask her to quit," Finola suggested.

For a moment Leah heard nothing but silence. Then Kay said, "I couldn't do that. Leah is still my friend."

Leah couldn't bear to hear any more. She gathered up her things and left the room, quietly closing the door behind her. She couldn't remember ever being so angry in her life—at least not since Pam Hunter had stolen her solo variation during the entrance auditions.

Sophie was right. What kind of world was this? Friends talking about friends behind each other's backs ... criticizing them. "Stiff," Leah muttered, her head down as she charged up the front stairs to the Blue Studio. She threw open the dressing-room door and was glad to see that she was the first to arrive. "Kay Larkin doesn't know the first thing about anything."

"Did you say something?" Pam said, walking in.

"No," Leah said fiercely. "I have nothing to say to anyone around here anymore." She sat down and violently pulled her high, red-suede character boots onto her feet, almost tearing the top off one of them.

"My, my!" Pam arched her eyebrows as she studied Leah in the mirror. "We're in a bad mood today."

"Yes, *we* are, Pam." Leah's voice was so cold that Pam, with a startled look, actually backed down and left her alone.

Leah walked into the classroom, still buttoning her skirt. She tossed her towel onto the nearest barre and sent her dance bag skittering across the floor, to land under the piano. She was tempted to confront Kay during rehearsal today. Leah would quit Kay's stupid ballet, quit the whole birthday gala—why, she'd quit the school if she could! But there was no need to. In a few weeks, or maybe in a few months' time at the latest, Leah had a feeling that she wouldn't be an SFBA student anymore. Madame had plans for her—not for Finola, not for Kay, not for Katrina—but for her, Leah Kimberly Stephenson. When she became the youngest member of the company, or even an apprentice, then they could talk about her all they wanted.

In the meantime, Leah wasn't going to give any of her so-called friends the chance to call her a quitter, behind her back *or* to her face. "Stiff," she muttered one more time. Then, grabbing the barre she did the highest battements she could. Her knees felt a little weird, but Leah didn't pay the least bit of attention. She pointed her toes and kicked her legs hard and high in the air. When all was said and done, what did Kay Larkin know about choreography—or friendship, for that matter? Leah thought, trying to ignore the tears building behind her eyes.

Chapter 11

On Sunday afternoon Pam voiced the question that had been on everyone's mind since class with Madame that morning. "Well, now that we've seen the prodigy in action, what's the verdict, folks?"

Leah hadn't said much of anything to anyone during the past week. Practicing late at school and working with Madame had given her the perfect excuse to miss group meals at Mrs. Hanson's, to skip lunch in the cafeteria, and to keep herself apart from the other girls in the usual round of chitchat preceding class. If her so-called friends wanted to think she was stuck up, then let them. Leah didn't care anymore.

Not that she had said so, not even once. She had been polite but distant, and just kept working, working, working—with Finola and, of course, with Kay. Kay had actually complimented her the night before and had told her she was beginning to get the feel of the music. Leah had thanked her coolly, then resumed practicing her two-second solo for Kay's as-yet untitled piece.

But now she glared at Pam over the open lid of the wardrobe trunk. She had promised Sophie she would be her friend, and Pam and the others had no right to talk about her like this. In an even voice, Leah said, "I think it's about time we stopped calling Sophie a prodigy and started treating her like a person!" Like everyone else in Madame's monthly Sunday class, Leah had been floored by Sophie. She was absolutely perfect. But Leah had decided that perfection wasn't something to run away from. Let everyone else envy Sophie; Leah was going to learn *from* her. "She's just a child," she went on, "a gifted child. I don't think you should be so hard on her."

"Pardon me!" Pam said with exaggerated politeness. "Of course you *are* in a slightly different position from the rest of us lowly souls."

Leah bristled, but Pam continued blithely, "She idolizes you—for some reason. And those bangs! She cut her bangs just like yours, Leah, and she looks ridiculous."

Leah's face flamed scarlet. Not so long ago Leah herself had had a crush on a famous ballerina: Lynne Vreeland, who later proved to be Kay's natural mother. Leah had cut her bangs to look like Lynne's and even dressed exactly like her for class. She had forgotten all about that until now. In her whole life, Leah had never felt so humiliated and embarrassed.

Kay surprised her by jumping to her rescue. "That's mean, Pam. We all do stuff like that. I once bought a whole new outfit to look like Gelsey Kirkland."

In spite of the coolness between them the past week, Leah smiled at Kay, grateful for her help.

But Pam refused to be put off. "Bangs aren't the point. Besides, I think Leah should take Sophie Potter more seriously. So far Leah's the only girl chosen around here to dance with the company and I heard a rumor"—Pam smiled benignly at Kay —"that Sophie may be taken right into the company without having to go to school here at all."

"That's not true! I know it isn't," Leah protested. "Madame wouldn't allow a twelve-year-old to be—"

"Exploited," Finola broke in. "Leah's right about that." She reached into the trunk and emerged with an armful of tattered blue tutus. She wrinkled her nose, shook out the limp skirts, then sneezed from the dust. She forced herself to examine them, then tossed the useless tulle garments on the nearest chair. For Madame's gala, nothing so shabby would do.

"Yes, but Madame is not in charge of the company!" Pam reminded them.

"You can say that again," Kay blurted out.

"What have you heard, Kay?" Finola asked eagerly.

Leah kept her eyes lowered on the skirt of her *Sick Chicken* costume. She held her breath and waited for Kay's answer.

"Nothing definite. Don't make me tell. I'll get into so much trouble," Kay pleaded.

'Since when did that bother our resident snoop!" Pam cried.

"This isn't the usual kind of gossip—it has to do with the company and the school, and I can't talk about it."

"A hint?" Katrina prodded.

"If you'll really get into trouble, don't say another word," Finola warned Kay.

Kay thought for a minute, then said carefully, "The school needs money badly, and so does the company."

"Money!" Pam tapped her longish, well-manicured nails against the dimple in her chin. "The root of all evil," she mused.

"And Sophie's box office, isn't she?" Finola said, sounding disappointed.

"Like Alex said," Leah whispered.

"What else did Alex say about Sophie?" Pam demanded.

"I bet Andrei told her some real insider information!" Kay's eyes grew wide in anticipation.

"Nothing," Leah said firmly. "Alex just said the same thing as Finola. That being only twelve, the poor kid would be a box-office draw that the benefactors couldn't and wouldn't resist. Something like that." Tossing her tutu aside, Leah stood up.

"Poor kid?" Kay said, as if she were amazed by Leah's choice of words.

Leah took a deep breath and whirled around. "Yes, the poor kid! She has no friends here yet. And after today do any of you really think she stands a chance of fitting in? Even girls in the *company* were looking at her like she was some kind of freak." A vision of small, delicate Sophie in class, floating across the floor like something out of a dream, filled Leah's head. Sophie's technique was so perfect that her dancing really looked effortless. "No wonder she cries herself to sleep," she murmured, then bit her lip. She had no right to betray Sophie that way.

The silence in the room was long and awkward. Finally Finola said softly, "Does Madame know this?"

"Of course not—I shouldn't have even mentioned it to you," Leah said sharply.

"Maybe not." Katrina sounded dubious. "But if someone's in trouble, not happy—"

Katrina broke off, and Leah knew why. Only a few days ago Katrina had said someone should tell Madame about Leah, too.

Kay slapped her hand against the sewing table in frustration. "This is all so gloomy! The kid's a great dancer. So what? I like her. I just haven't had a chance to get to know her. In another week she'll be here as a regular student. I think we're jumping the gun," she said confidently. "I think she'll fit in just fine, especially if we work on it." Then Kay held up the boy's bolero jacket that she'd been sewing. New sequins brightened the slightly worn fabric that Marc would wear for his *Don Quixote* pas de deux with Pam. "Too bad for Sophie—and for me," she continued, "that she can't be part of the gala." She dropped her hands into her lap and stared dreamily into space. "She's the most *natural* dancer I've ever seen."

"Natural?" Pam looked dubious. "I don't know about that. She's well *trained*."

"But she seems to absorb technique like some kind of sponge," Kay said.

"Like the earth soaks up rain," Finola agreed. "Yes, that is how she moves. That's what makes her different."

"I'd give my right arm to have her dance in my piece—all that training, and yet none of it gets in the way of how she moves!" Kay observed.

"The opposite of me, in other words," Leah said, a bit shrilly. "Isn't it? It's what you said was *wrong* with my dancing. You'd rather have Sophie in my part, wouldn't you?"

"And this is the person who's not going to be jealous of the kid!" Pam reminded them, laughing.

"I'm not jealous, not at all. I'm just upset with Kay. I thought friendship counted for something around here, but from what I've seen lately, it doesn't," Leah said angrily.

"Leah!" Kay exclaimed. "This has nothing to do with you. You're a different sort of dancer from Sophie, yes. But I wouldn't use her the same way I'm using you."

Leah was too upset to see the difference. "Sorry, Kay, I don't get it. You have been telling me all along I'm stiff—"

"You're looser than you were," Kay interjected.

"Right, Kay. Looser than I *was*. But tell the truth. You'd rather use Sophie than me."

"It's not an either-or sort of thing," Kay declared, shaking her head at Leah. "The trouble with you is that you're too stiff—in the head! I bet you haven't seen more than five modern dance performances in your whole life—let alone experimental stuff like what I'm trying to do."

"No, I haven't. When would I have time to?" Leah countered.

"Tonight, for instance. Remember that workshop I told you about? Of all the people here, you're the one who should see this woman at work. You should check it out. But no, you can't—or rather, you won't."

"Of course I can't! I have rehearsal with Madame, and then I'll just be too tired, Kay. You're not making sense. And besides," Leah was practically shouting now, "I'm not ever going to be a modern dancer."

"No one said you were!" Kay declared hotly. "But you are one of the best dancers I've ever seen, except that you keep limiting yourself. If you want to be a great ballerina these days, you can't just prance around in tutus and on pointe. You've got to understand other kinds of movement. This is almost the twenty-first century!" Kay cried, rather dramatically.

"I don't have to listen to this. And besides, I don't have the time." Leah looked at the clock. She had exactly half an hour to race down to the Opera House for the dress rehearsal of *Dance Indigo*.

Kay shook her head in disgust. "Okay, but it's your loss, not mine."

"That's right, Kay. Just keep that in mind," Leah said, flouncing out the door. She slammed it shut behind her, but not fast enough to drown out Pam Hunter's surprised drawl.

"What in the world's getting into *her?*"

Chapter 12

    "And what, Leah, do you think you're doing?"* Madame's voice was so loud that it echoed off the top balcony of the Opera House.

Leah stumbled off pointe and instinctively stepped closer to Patrick. She blinked back the sweat dripping off her forehead into her eyes, and wondered if she was actually supposed to answer Madame or just stand there getting yelled at.

For a moment the only sounds in the huge auditorium seemed to be the *thump, thump, thump* of her heart and the bang of a stagehand's hammer as he nailed something together in the wings.

Madame made a small sound of disgust, then rose from her front-row seat and actually stomped up the side steps leading onto the stage.

"We have rehearsed this combination how many times now?"

Leah figured this was a question to be answered, the way Madame tapped her foot against the floor.

"A lot," she said in a very small voice. She clutched the plain white skirt of her costume. She couldn't help but wonder exactly what she'd done wrong. Frantically she went through the steps in her head. As far as she could tell, she hadn't missed one.

"You're moving like some kind of robot." Madame stopped talking and launched into a stilted, rather cruelly exaggerated version of Leah's preparation for the jump into Patrick's arms. "Again!" She waved her hand at the conductor, who was seated at the piano in the orchestra pit, and stayed right onstage.

Leah counted two bars, then began again. She glided across the floor, trying to make the steps flow into each other. She winced when she stubbed her toe on one of the floorboards but just kept going, anyway. In her hand she was counting, Glissade, two three, inside turn, developpé, double turn, attitude, then she jumped into Patrick's arms.

Her preparation plié wasn't deep enough, and she murmured "Sorry" under her breath. She could feel Patrick's arms shaking as he struggled to get her above his head.

"Patrick," Madame remarked coldly. "Leah is not a very big girl. You are lifting her like she's a sack of potatoes! Never, ever make a girl look bad onstage. You must always make her look as light as a feather. That's your job." Then Madame stalked over to the orchestra pit and chided the conductor for taking the passage too fast. "The girl needs more time for preparation; slow the tempo to this ..." She paused to clap out the rhythm with her hands.

Patrick sighed as he put Leah down, then flashed

her a tired grin. "Don't look so surprised. She yells at *everyone* during rehearsals. She's very tense about this one. *Dance Indigo* is her baby."

Leah couldn't help but be shocked. She hadn't expected Madame to treat company principals the same way she treated the girls in her class.

"But we're falling apart," Leah said despairingly. She dropped to the floor and massaged her aching knees. "Two days more and then it's the real thing." Her voice trembled.

Crouching down beside her, Patrick lifted her face toward his. "Hey, it's par for the course. Dress rehearsals are notoriously awful—particularly when one of the principals is one hour late." He cast a rueful glance toward the wings. Ashley was nowhere in sight.

"I'm surprised Madame puts up with her," Leah said.

"Madame has no choice. Ashley is Edgar Roth's pick of the week. She's hot right now, and the company big shots want her on the program in a piece that's sure to get a good review. Besides, she is a wonderful dancer! So all the company politics don't really matter in her case."

Patrick smiled at Leah. "I keep forgetting you're new to all of this. Well, don't worry so much about it, Leah. Company problems have very little to do with you, at this point in your life."

If only they did! Leah responded in her head. Every day she waited for Madame to take her aside and tell her about performing Juliet with the touring company. On the other hand, company politics sounded far worse than the competition that raged around the Academy. Leah suddenly wondered if she was ready to brave the storms of the real dance world.

Madame finished with the conductor and, brushing off her pale tailored wool slacks, faced her dancers again. "Let's take it from the top—oh, hello. I suppose later is better than never?"

Leah and Patrick turned around. Ashley was standing in the wings peeling off her leg warmers. "Sorry, Madame, wardrobe had a problem with this costume." She turned around and displayed the back of her low-cut red dress. Wide white basting stitches ran up along the side of the zipper closure.

"We were just about to start again." Madame sounded worn out. "Leah, enter stage left." Madame commanded Patrick and Ashley into the wings with a clap of her hands. "And this time, Stephenson, put more energy into it. You are dancing today with the enthusiasm of an overcooked noodle. Are you feeling all right?"

"I'm fine, Madame," Leah replied in a tired voice. "Just fine."

Leah was halfway across the stage in her opening combination. For the first time that afternoon, her turns were quick enough and centered, and she felt the music filling her. Coming out of her last pirouette, she lost her spot: a white lightbulb hanging in the wings. A man in a suit and street shoes was parading across the stage right in front of her. Leah tried to catch herself, but her leg skidded out from under her and she landed hard on her behind.

She let out a yelp, then scrambled to her feet just as Patrick reached her. "Are you okay?" he asked, his face taut with worry.

Madame pushed past the other man and helped brush Leah off. "You could have been hurt! You lost your spot, didn't you?"

"Yes," Leah said tightly, and glared at the short-ish, balding man. He was standing by the orchestra stairs, and he gave Leah a bland smile. Obviously he had no idea he had almost caused a disaster. Leah walked around in a circle, kicking out her legs, trying to make the ache in her hip go away.

"Keep moving," Madame told her, "but take a break."

"Madame Preston, if your dancer is all right, I must talk to you—now!"

At the man's commanding tone, Leah looked up. She'd never heard anyone order Madame around before.

Madame's shoulders tensed visibly and she paused to compose herself before facing him. "If I'm not back in five minutes," she said to Patrick, "take over. Run through the whole piece one more time at least. But whatever this nonsense is, it shouldn't take long."

Then she followed the man down the orchestra stairs. They sat down in the front row and started talking in hushed voices.

"Who is that?" Leah asked as Ashley handed her a glass of water.

"Roth, Edgar Roth. He's the acting company director while Robin Mosely is off in Paris,"

Ashley said. "I can't imagine what he's doing here. Madame does not like him," she confided. "And I don't blame her."

Leah thought that was strange, considering Mr. Roth had just given Ashley a big break.

"Are you ready to go on now?" Patrick asked after glancing at his watch. "The lighting crew needs to check us one more time, and now that Ashley is here, we can run straight through without stopping."

Leah put her glass of water in the wings, and Patrick stayed onstage long enough to tell the conductor to start. Leah launched into the dance again. Her entrance wasn't as smooth, but for the first time since learning the steps, she felt the shape of the beginning phrases.

"Good, Leah!" Patrick cried as she flung herself toward him. Then she was in his arms, her hands wrapped around his neck as he spun her around in a circle. When he put her down, her legs felt unusually tired and weak, but she forced herself to pretend that she was strong. Then Ashley came on, and Leah lingered in the wings, dabbing the sweat off her shoulders with a towel. She watched Ashley entice Patrick in a sultry pas de deux, then as the music shifted she listened for her cue. She almost missed the chords because of the loud voices coming from the front of the stage.

Onstage, the argument raging in the front row of the orchestra was even clearer. Patrick turned Leah around in a supported arabesque, but she stopped before going on to the next set of steps. Patrick looked at her, confused for a minute. Then he heard Madame, too. He stopped, and the piano followed suit.

"I will not take Leah out of this ballet, and that's my final decision. You cannot threaten me, Edgar Roth. I am in charge of my dancers' well-being. It is important to Leah *and* to Sophie Potter that Leah dance in this partiuclar piece at this time."

"Take me out!" Leah gasped, and turned helplessly to Patrick. "What's going on?"

Patrick's kind face was creased in a frown. "I'm not sure," he said under his breath, "but I don't think we're supposed to hear this." He started to motion toward the orchestra pit again, but Leah reached up and grabbed his hand.

"You bet your life I'm going to hear this. It's me they're talking about. Madame's going to let him take me out of the ballet," Leah said, her voice rising to a hysterical pitch. She marched out to the apron of the stage and shielded her eyes from the bright lights.

"Madame?" she called, not quite able to locate the source of the voices. "Is something wrong?"

"Now look what you've done!" Madame cried, and started up the steps toward Leah. Mr. Roth was right behind her.

"*I* haven't done a thing." He was waving the entertainment section of the day's paper at Madame. "The press has. The public is ready for Sophie Potter. Certainly a prodigy can dance an easy thing like this. I want her in the company *now*. I want her in *Dance Indigo* Wednesday, and that's my final word."

Madame arrived at Leah's side. "Go to the dressing room," she told her, then turned back to Mr. Roth. "I will not discuss this further. Leah will perform on Wednesday."

"Leah is no prodigy. She hasn't had the same kind of press, and we need the publicity. You artists always refuse to understand the practical end of things. Then you come crying when there's no money to keep the company going!" Mr. Roth argued.

"Stop!" Leah screamed. "You people are the most awful, cruelest, rudest people I have ever met in my life!" she accused a startled Mr. Roth. "I am not a piece of meat. I am not a statue. I am a human being, and you have no right to discuss me and my future and my whole life like this as if I don't exist. You can have your dumb ballet, Madame," Leah spat. "I quit. I've had it with dancing, and with this whole stupid company and school and—" Whatever else Leah would have said was strangled by her tears. With her hand over her mouth, she fled from the stage. Sobbing, she pushed past the stagehands and startled dancers who had gathered in the wings at the sound of angry voices. Her toe shoes clunked against the metal steps as she ran the whole way down to the dressing room where she had stashed her clothes.

Leah sank down in the chair and stared at her tear-streaked face in the mirror. Her heavy eye makeup had run, and tears poured like muddy rivers down her cheeks. All that hard work, all that determination—and it ended like this, with

Madame right in front of her talking about her as if she were some kind of object. As if she didn't have ears! Leah buried her face in her arms and sobbed.

"Leah?" Madame said softly. Leah hadn't heard her come in, but she could sense the director standing right behind her chair, waiting for her to apologize.

"I'm not sorry, Madame, I'm not," Leah mumbled. Then she sat up straight. Leah's haunted eyes met Madame's reflection in the mirror. "I'm not sorry at all," she repeated in a trembling voice. "That man had no right to interrupt us. He had no right to talk about me like that—to make all this work I've done look useless. What does he know, anyway?"

Madame shrugged and pulled up a chair next to Leah's. She pushed the tangle of tights onto the floor and perched on the edge of the seat.

Before Madame could say anything, Leah got up. "I meant what I said. I won't dance in this ballet—or anything else for that matter. It's just not worth it." She looked directly into Madame's steely gray eyes. She had to make Madame see that she was telling the truth. She was speaking from the bottom of her heart. Dance for Leah Stephenson was over and done with. Being treated like some kind of hired hand was not what she had worked so hard for. San Lorenzo, here I come, she thought, and was surprised at the relief that coursed through her. I'm that tired, she realized.

"Sit down, Leah." Madame patted the chair. "Let's try to calm down before we discuss this. All right?" Leah hesitated, then her eyes faltered beneath Madame's steady gaze. She obeyed and sank down into the chair, but kept her back straight and her hands folded tightly in her lap. Leah wanted to tell Madame she was already calm enough and that there was really nothing to discuss. The ballet could very well go on without her—the steps were so easy, Sophie could learn the whole piece in a matter of hours!

"Mr. Roth is acting company director," Madame said, looking down at her hands.

"I will not apologize!" Leah was adamant.

"No—and besides, I will deal with Mr. Roth. But you have made a commitment."

"*I've* made a commitment?" Leah jumped up again. She marched across the small dressing room and stood facing the wardrobe rack. "You gave me this part, Madame Preston." She turned around and confronted her teacher. "I've worked harder than you'll ever know to learn it. I've worked harder than I have in my life the past couple of weeks just to prove to you that I'm worth it." Leah's voice started to shake again. She tried to pull herself together, but everything inside her head was like a puzzle with pieces that didn't fit together: her problems with Kay, Sophie's arrival, the way the other girls were treating her....

Madame cleared her throat. "Leah, why do you think I gave this part to you?"

Leah hadn't expected that question. "Because ..." She paused and reviewed the events of the past week in her head. "Because you wanted Alex—you wanted Alex for this, and for Juliet, and for everything, and she let you down by leaving. I was your next best bet."

Madame's thin lips parted slightly in surprise. "Leah, you are not my next best anything! You were the best girl for the job. Ashley was wrong for that role, and Diana, as you know, was unavailable. No one else was right. I wanted the best possible person for this ballet. Don't forget, *I'm* the choreographer. I want my steps to be worn well...." She searched her mind for an image and actually smiled. "I think of it as someone like Dior having a favorite person in mind to wear a particular dress he designed. You fit the bill—perfectly, Leah."

A lump seemed to form in Leah's throat. Those were the words she'd been waiting to hear for weeks now. Finally she squeaked out a meek, "I do? Perfectly?"

"Yes," Madame assured her. She motioned for Leah to come back over to the dressing table. Leah hesitated, then sat down again. Gently, Madame began to take the hairpins out of Leah's hair. Then she picked up a brush, and tears brimmed out of Leah's eyes. A few nights ago, she had brushed Sophie's hair just like this because it had seemed the most natural way to calm a little girl down. To Madame, Leah found herself thinking, we're all little girls.

"What you said about Alex—yes, I am very disappointed in her and I haven't quite given up on the idea of her dancing. Not yet."

"But she left school and I don't even know if she's taking classes and—"

"She's taking classes," Madame said, nodding her head. "In Berkeley, at a local studio. She doesn't know that the teacher, Anne Stevens, is a friend of mine." Madame almost smiled. Then she turned Leah toward her. "That looks better." She put the brush down and pushed Leah's bangs out of her eyes. "Alex has dance in her blood. What *kind* of dance and what she does with it next, who knows? She is so temperamental." Madame gave a small shrug.

"Now, what was this about Juliet?" Madame folded her hands in her lap and waited for an answer.

"Well ..." Leah decided to get everything out in the open; that was the only way she'd know if it was true or not. "Alex was supposed to dance it, right? But someone told me that you were going to cast me in the part instead, with the touring company, because she was gone. And then I heard that Sophie would get the part instead of me."

"Someone told you *that!*" Madame looked perfectly astounded. "All that?"

Leah's heart sank at Madame's surprised reaction.

"It's not true, Leah. Not yet, anyway. Maybe in a year or so you can dance Juliet with the touring company—no promises, though," Madame added quickly.

"Next month, next year—Oh, Madame!" Leah cried joyfully. "As long as I know it's not years and years away."

"But you gave up your dancing and everything just now," Madame reminded her with a hint of the old sternness in her voice.

Leah squirmed in her chair. "I felt ... I felt humiliated."

"Well, that's not surprising. And as I said, I will deal with Mr. Roth. That is part of my job. And as for you, your job is getting some rest and then dancing your best on Wednesday. If you still want to give up dancing after that, I'll think about accepting your resignation." Madame's face was prefectly serious, but then her mouth broke into a grin.

"But what about Sophie? People do want to see her. She's incredible! Everyone thinks she won't be at the school long and will be in the company—well, soon."

"Sophie is my business, Leah," Madame said tightly, and rose from her chair. With dignity, she handed Leah her street clothes. "Not yours or anyone else's at the Academy. You might pass that word around for me."

"Yes, Madame," Leah obeyed, lowering her eyes. But as Madame headed for the door, Leah leapt to her feet and rushed up to her. She wanted to throw her arms around Madame's neck and kiss her, but she stopped herself in time. Madame was not the type to be hugged. Instead, Leah would have to communicate her gratitude in words. "Thank you, Madame. I promise you you won't be sorry you gave me this chance."

Ten minutes later Leah was near the stage door shouting into the pay phone. "Kay, it's me!" Leah was breathless. "Do you still have those tickets for the choreography workshop this evening? Can I go with you?"

Kay paused for an excruciatingly long moment on the other end. "What changed your mind?" She sounded strangely cautious.

Leah closed her eyes. Was it too late? "What you said today about if I want to be a great dancer—it sank in. I do want to be a great dancer. I'm not going to quit—"

"Quit? You, *quit*?" Kay's laugh was almost harsh. "I never said you were quitting."

"Oh, it's too much to explain now. Let's just say I came to my senses, and if it's not too late, I'd like to join you. I'd like to do my best in your ballet. I'd like to understand better what it is you do."

Kay laughed her old familiar, cheerful laugh. "You take the cake, Stephenson. I've never seen anyone go through so many strange moods in one week in my entire life! But you're in luck. No one else wanted that ticket, either. There's a case of terminal gala exhaustion going on around here. I'm surprised you're not too tired to go." Then they made plans to meet at the old church in the Haight that had been converted into an experimental dance and performance space.

Kay had come quite close to the truth, though. Leah was more exhausted than she had ever been before, but she figured she could weather a few more days of hard work. Coming so close to abandoning her dream of being a ballerina had scared her. Scared me right *into* my senses, she thought as she rushed for the bus.

Madame had said that she didn't want her in the company yet, and Leah felt a strange sense of relief at that thought.

Someday, in the not too distant future, Leah could be Juliet. Probably in some small California town, in front of an audience that would whistle at Leah's legs, she'd dance her first full-length role. But after her talk with Madame tonight, that was fine with Leah. Madame had told her she was perfect for *Dance Indigo.* She could subsist on that compliment for months.

And now she knew what really mattered to her. She wanted to be a great dancer—nothing more, nothing less.

Chapter 13

Dana Daniels, the choreographer,
looked like a person who lived on black coffee
and bean sprouts. Clad in a shapeless black
jumpsuit, she was short and extremely thin. Her
hair was cut like a boy's, short and spiky on top,
and she wore absolutely no makeup. Leah sat on
the crowded floor of the new Arts Spark performance space down in the Haight and wondered
how she'd survive five minutes, never mind an
hour, of demonstrations by this sullen-faced
person.

Then Dana Daniels smiled. She had the warmest,
brightest smile Leah had ever seen. It was like the
burst of dawn after a dark, stormy night. Alex
would love this person! Leah thought, and hoped
they would meet someday because Leah could
see that, like Alex, Dana Daniels ran deep.

Dana began the workshop by introducing herself. She was from New York, and her background
in dance was completely different from anything
Leah had ever suspected: ballet, martial arts, yoga,
various sports, and gymnastics as well as several
versions of modern technique.

"Movement's what you make it," she said in her sharp, staccato voice. Every word she spoke seemed to be punctuated by an expressive gesture using her face, body, or hands. Even her large green eyes seemed to dance. "What we'll do here today is probably different from anything any of you are used to." She glanced around the room, and Leah suddenly felt self-conscious about her perfect ballet dancer's body. "But that's good for me—and you, too. No preconceptions. Now let's get started. Talking about dance never works in the end."

Leah would have held back, but Kay grabbed her hand and made sure that they were in the first group of people called up to join the opening improvisation. Working with Kay hadn't quite prepared Leah for this. Kay had made her dancers think of circles, and circles were something Leah and everyone else had seen. Dana, however, was light-years beyond circles.

She asked her dancers to be sharp or curved or to move like something broken, and at the same time to make their own rhythm. She quickly demonstrated stamps, hand claps, and even shouts. Leah had never felt so stupid in her life. It seemed Dana wanted them to look like sculpture—moving sculpture—of the modern kind. Leah felt like a dumb blonde who only knew how to pose for the camera. She felt the only sculpture she could be was one of Degas's ballerinas! She watched Kay out of the corner of her eye, wishing she had the nerve to copy her. Kay was very good, Leah realized. At the moment her body suggested the curve in a road as she slithered across the floor.

"You must be a ballerina!" Dana said to Leah. She studied Leah's body. "Go with what you do best. Remember, all movement is dancing. You have a particular kind of movement, quiet and balanced. Why don't you think of a movement that is actually still? Find the rhythm in being still." Then Dana moved on. Leah stood a moment, very still and stunned. "Use it," Dana had implied. Not "Change it." "Don't fight yourself," Dana said to someone else, but her eyes met Leah's and she winked.

Leah took a deep breath and thought of the most solid, still thing she could. The first picture that came to her mind was of a mountain. Leah lifted her arms very slowly into what felt like a peak. Then she let her body curve—that was the second part of the assignment—to make something sharp into something curved. Leah collapsed onto the floor but didn't move an inch from the spot where she'd started. Then she thought of mountains and how they grow and wear down and then probably begin all over again. Before she knew it, she was making the beginnings of a dance.

"To think I almost didn't come!" Leah said after she and Kay climbed into the bus to head home. It was past eight, and Leah should have been in her bath an hour ago, and her feet were actually throbbing. But she was too excited to care. She turned and faced her friend. "I think I really understand modern dance!"

"I think you do, too," Kay said quietly. She sounded preoccupied. "Leah, I've got an idea, but you're going to have to learn something pretty fast."

Leah had to laugh. "What else is new these days?" She stuck her legs out in front of her and studied their shape through her jeans. For the first time in her life, she felt as though she really knew her body. After all her years of dancing, she hadn't ever thought of how *she* moved. She was always too worried about how movements were supposed to be *done*. Leah settled back in her seat and stifled a giggle. What if she actually became a modern dancer someday? What would Kay say then?

Kay was lost in her own thoughts. "Of course we can't go to school now, it's closed, and we'll only have a little time in the morning—"

"Oh, no, those wheels are churning." Leah regarded Kay with great affection. She had missed being friends. She had missed this kind of time with all of her friends: talking, breathing, and sleeping dance. Without Finola, Kay, Katrina, and Linda to share it with, life as a dancer had seemed very cold and lonely.

"Tonight in your room ... before I lose my inspiration," Kay said.

"In my room?" Leah sat up straighter. She tucked her bangs under her beret and pulled her scarf tighter around her neck. "You don't intend to start choreographing something for me in my room—tonight?"

Kay didn't answer. She was tapping her finger against the palm of her opposite hand. Try as she might, Leah couldn't worm one more word out of Kay.

* * *

After a late supper, Leah spent an hour with Sophie helping her plan how to redecorate her room. Then, dizzy with exhaustion, she dragged herself upstairs to wait for Kay. It was after eleven-thirty when Kay finally knocked on Leah's door.

She poked her curly head in the door and put a finger to her lips. "Now, this is the plan." She frowned at Leah's nightgown. "You can't practice in that!"

"Practice, here? Now?" Leah eyed her sore feet. "Kay, it's *so* late."

"Yes, I know." Kay had that serious look on her face that she always got when she was really in-spired. "And we'll be working on pointe, Leah," she said. "Fortunately, no one sleeps right below you."

Leah didn't even try to protest. She slipped on some tights and pulled an oversized T-shirt over her head. With a great sigh, she picked a pair of pointe shoes out of the stash by the window and put them on. "Why pointe work; why now?" she asked.

"Well, you know what Dana said to you, about doing what you do best. You're the best classical ballet dancer in the school, so why fight it? We should use it. Only we'll use it in a different way."

Leah grinned. "That's what I said right at the beginning of our rehearsals," she reminded Kay.

"Yes, but I wasn't listening." Kay didn't seem bothered by that fact at all. "And you had the wrong attitude. You thought ballet was something *better* than whatever other dance we were trying to do. It isn't. But I think that if what I have in mind works, you, Leah, are going to steal the show as usual."

For the next two hours, Kay coached Leah. The hardest part was not the pointe work but the laughter. Kay cracked up completely. On the one hand, she was mocking every ballet cliché in the repertoire. On the other hand, Kay's method of stringing different steps together actually worked, in the end creating five minutes of incredibly difficult but interesting dancing.

"Can you do it?" Kay asked. She was flat on Leah's bed, her eyes bloodshot with exhaustion. Her hand was holding the alarm clock. Ever since they had stopped rehearsing, Kay had been lying like that, too weak to even look at the time.

"I'll do it!" Leah promised. Kay's energy had inspired her, and she loved the fact that Kay had given her the best choreography in the hour-long program of pieces for Madame's party. Leah would steal the show, and Madame wouldn't be sorry she'd stuck by her.

Just as Leah wasn't sorry she'd stuck it out with Kay. With great effort, Leah lifted her head and looked at Kay from her vantage point on the chair. Kay had fallen asleep, still in her sweatpants and holding the alarm clock in a limp hand. Leah managed a weak grin. She'd tell Kay how grateful she was for her help in the morning. For now she'd let her sleep right there on her bed. Leah was so exhausted that she fell asleep sitting up in her chair.

Chapter 14

The night of Madame's birthday gala had finally arrived, and for five precious minutes Leah had the small dressing room behind the auditorium stage all to herself. Peering into the cracked old mirror above the dressing table, Leah put the finishing touches on her mascara and checked her makeup one last time.

Leah's hair was still undone, and the oversized, gaudy pink tutu she and Kay had pieced together for Kay's dance hung over the back of a chair. Leah had to be dressed and ready for curtain time even though *Footprints,* as Kay had dubbed it, was midway through the program. Leah and Kay were still convinced that the short solo would steal the show.

In front of her on the table was the growing collection of knickknacks and lucky charms that Leah always brought with her before any performance: the rabbit's foot Andrei had given her, Alex's beaded bag, and a small framed photo of Margot Fonteyn. It was a picture Leah had carefully clipped from a magazine when she was ten years old. It showed five-year-old Fonteyn in a tutu standing in a perfect arabesque. As a child, Fonteyn had had the same perfect balance and line that she had had as a great and mature ballerina. Glued to the back of the frame was part of an interview Leah had recently photocopied in the library. It was something Madame had quoted back during the entrance auditions in September. Dame Margot Fonteyn had once said that in order to be a great artist, you had to have only good in your heart.

Leah took a deep breath. If only she were able to remember that. She had been so angry the past couple of weeks—at Madame, at Alex, certainly at Kay, and, it seemed, at almost everyone else in the small world of SFBA.

Leah felt she had something very important to say to Kay before the gala started, before the excitement swept everyone off their feet. She wanted Finola to hear it, too. She quickly fixed her hair, stepped into her ridiculous tutu, and hooked up the back as far as she could reach. Then, after pulling on her leg warmers, she hurried out of the dressing room.

Kay was standing onstage, chewing the eraser of a pencil. She had plastic warm-up pants over her tights and someone's *Temptations* sweatshirt tied by its sleeves around her neck. Finola was pacing the floor in front of her. It was hard to say which girl looked more nervous.

"Hi!" Leah said. Finola's eyes bulged at the sight of Leah's tutu. Leah presented her back, and Finola finished hooking it up.

"How in the world will you dance in that?"

Finola asked, aghast. "I hope you rehearsed in it. It's so heavy." Dubiously, she fingered the enormously full tulle, satin, and brocade skirt.

"What do you think we are, Finola, rank amateurs?" Kay pretended to look insulted.

Leah just laughed. "We rehearsed enough."

"Well, good luck, anyway!" Finola said cheerfully, and began to walk away.

"Wait!" Leah cried. "I want to talk to you." Smiling at Kay, she added, "And you, too."

Finola frowned. "Is something wrong?"

"No, I just wanted to say, to both of you, that I'm sorry."

"Sorry?" Kay blinked. "Hey, whatever happened in the past couple of weeks is over with, finished, finito ..." She turned to Finola.

"Passé?" Finola suggested. "Old history?"

Leah didn't want to let them joke about it. "I know it's over with. And I felt better after Sunday, after going with you to see Dana Daniels, and after working out this new part of your dance. But I was wrong about a lot of things," Leah admitted.

Switching her clipboard to her right hand, Finola reached out and hugged Leah. "Tonight's no time for apologies. It's time to dance."

"Yes, but I wanted to say it, anyway. Please don't stop me," Leah begged, and something in her face must have warned the other girls how important—and how difficult—it was for her to say what she was about to say.

"Pam was right. My nose has been stuck up in the air ever since I learned that I was to perform in *Dance Indigo*. I was so stupid. I thought I had outgrown needing this place, and my classes and my friends."

"Oh, Leah, but I know you didn't really *believe* all that!" Kay cried.

"But I did, Kay, I did. I didn't take you seriously enough, and you're one of the most serious artists in this whole school. And you knew what I had almost forgotten—which is that you never, ever stop learning."

Kay's reaction surprised Leah. She didn't throw her arms around her or hug her or crack a joke. Instead, her deep blue eyes merely darkened with emotion and she nodded. "Thanks, Leah, I really do appreciate that," she said.

"Me, too, love," Finola added. Then someone called to her from the wings.

Kay wished Leah luck, then hurried off to attend to her own costume.

Leah squeezed herself past the other kids warming up in the wings and shrugged off her shawl. Back onstage, Kenny was on a ladder changing the gel on one of the lights.

"Don't walk under this!" Kenny warned with a laugh.

"I'm not the superstitious type!" Leah bantered, and batted one of the rungs as she walked by. She realized that she felt happier than she had in days. The pressure was almost over; what she felt now—the familiar swish of butterflies in her stomach as she circled the stage with her hands on her hips, testing the floor—wasn't pressure. It was the pre-performance jitters that she had grown to look forward to and, in a funny way, even love. She had learned in the past few months that a bad case of nerves before curtain time revved her up to peak level for the show.

But the pressure of working to prove herself to Madame, to Kay—and probably most of all to Leah Stephenson—suddenly seemed to be gone. She felt as if she'd been through some kind of trial by fire and had passed the test. Tomorrow she and everyone else would see what the real Leah Stephenson was made of, and no one, not even Mr. Roth, would wish Sophie Potter had been chosen for *Dance Indigo.*

As for tonight, Leah was determined to have fun. If she knew her audience as well as she thought she did, she'd have them doubled over in their seats, laughing. The thought of Madame with the giggles made Leah grin as she kicked out a kink in her knee. She pulled her purple leg warmers up higher while Kenny removed the ladder. Then Leah began to mark her solo for *Footprints.*

The oversized tutu was heavier than she remembered from yesterday's dress rehearsal, and the skirt tended to sag over her slim hips. Leah frowned as she looked down at the layers and layers of tulle and satin and beading. She'd have to have Finola help her baste the waist before the performance. The costume weighed a ton, and for just an instant, Leah regretted not having had the chance to practice in it one more time.

Then Marc and Michael came onstage, barefoot, wearing jeans and loose cotton shirts with rolled-up sleeves. To the left of Leah, they began practicing the series of lifts and leapfrogging motions, first Michael over Marc's head, then Marc over Michael's. They were well paired, both slim, dark, and graceful in a way that Leah hadn't really noticed before. It was a new idea for Leah, two guys dancing a pas de deux together. There was amazing strength to it, and something quirky, too—the same jarring feeling that ran through Kay's whole piece. Unexpected combinations of steps, of people, of costumes. Kay was going to be a great choreographer, Leah thought. No, she told herself, Kay *is* a great choreographer. Leah went back to marking her variation on the stage.

"Floor's slick!" Michael complained from somewhere behind her. Leah had been thinking the same thing. She carefully went up on pointe and did a bourrée forward to test the surface. To her surprise, the darning on the tips of her shoes didn't seem to help much. She rubbed her backside tenderly. The spot where she had fallen on Sunday was all bruised. She then circled the smooth floor on pointe one more time to get the feel of the surface. Dancing on pointe without rosin was certainly going to be tricky. It hadn't felt bad when she and Kay had rehearsed down in the gym, but the auditorium stage slanted downhill a bit toward the audience. Finola had told everyone that stages in Europe were often built like this on purpose, but Kay was convinced that here in San Francisco the tilt had more to do with the San Andreas Fault and earthquakes.

"How's it feel?" Katrina asked over the noise beginning to filter back through the drawn curtain. The auditorium was filling up, and there were only a few minutes left until the show began.

"Not bad," Leah said. She came off pointe, walked over to her starting postion, and danced the first few measures full-out: strange, bent-leg pirouettes, inside first, then outside. A couple of gliding connecting steps. Then a triple attitude turn. Forgetting about the floor, Leah threw herself into the movement. Her heavy tutu seemed to drag in the air. Leah's timing was slightly off as she found her spot. Her head whipped round, once, twice—and then suddenly she felt her leg go out from under her.

"Leah!" Katrina screamed, just as Leah crumpled to the floor.

Something seemed to snap inside her foot. Leah lay for a moment, dazed. "I'm okay," she started to say. She leaned back on her elbows to help hoist herself up. But as she put her foot to the floor, a terrible pain shot up her left leg, from her toes all the way to her hip.

And then she blacked out.

Leah lay perfectly still, trying to figure out where she had smelled that particular scent before. It wasn't the scent of hairspray or the pancake makeup she used before every performance or the soap she used every morning.

"She's coming around!" a soft voice said, and Leah recognized it as belonging to someone she knew.

She opened her eyes slowly, but the lights were so bright it hurt to look up. Why was she lying onstage, under the spotlights, like this? she wondered. Then she remembered: the smell was like the one from the time when she was about nine and had broken her arm and had to go to the hospital.

"Where am I?" Leah tried to ask, but her voice came out all slurred. Her tongue felt fuzzy, and she was very thirsty.

"You're okay, Leah," someone told her.

"Madame?" Leah tried to sit up, but hands gently pressed her back down. Madame's face came into focus, and then behind her was Alex and some people in white coats. Michael Litvak was there, too. His stage makeup looked very strange under the bright lights, and his eyes were shining. He looked as if he had been crying. Alex walked closer to her and squeezed Leah's hand hard.

"I know you are wondering what I am doing here. I came to see you dance."

Leah reached down to smooth her tutu, but it was gone. "Where's my costume?" she asked them, beginning to panic. "Where am I?"

"You're at the hospital, Leah. You're going to be fine," said a man in a white coat. His voice was so even and calm that his words sounded like a lullaby. But it wasn't the kind of lullaby that soothed Leah—it was the way people talked to her when they were lying, when they didn't want to tell you something.

Leah tried to get her thoughts together. She looked back up at him. He was a young man, and Leah thought how cute he looked standing next to Alex. They made a nice couple. Leah passed her hand over her face. What was she thinking? She fixed her eyes on the tag the man was wearing on his pocket. It said: Dr. Demuth. "You're a doctor," she observed. "But I can't see a doctor now, I have a performance." Her hands felt for her tutu again. "What happened? Why won't anyone answer me?"

Madame cleared her throat and looked uneasily at the doctor, then turned back to Leah. She tried to smile. "You took a bad fall on the stage, Leah."

"But I have to dance for your gala," Leah began. She stared at Madame. "What are you doing here?" Leah's throat felt so dry she could barely get the words out. "Today's your birthday and there's a big surprise planned, and tomorrow I have to be able to dance. The performance ..." Leah's voice began to shake. She tried to sit up again, but she felt as if her legs weren't attached to her, and when she moved the whole room started to spin.

"Leah, you are going to be all right, but you can't dance tonight and you won't be able to dance tomorrow," Madame explained. "Kay put Sophie in the piece tonight, and tomorrow we've made arrangements for Diana."

Alex just kept looking at Leah with the saddest eyes and squeezing her hand tightly.

Suddenly, Leah realized that Kay and Finola weren't in the room; that meant the performance must still be going on. She must have fallen and ruined the gala for Madame! Tears brimmed out of her eyes.

"I don't think you should worry her with this now, Madame Preston," Dr. Demuth said.

"Perhaps, but I think Leah would be more worried if she thought the show didn't go on."

"Yes—yes, but when can I dance again?" Leah asked. She felt so weak, and her eyes were so heavy. They must have given her medicine to sleep, she thought, to take away whatever was hurting. But she wouldn't go to sleep unless she knew she could move her legs. She bit her lip and tried as hard as she could. Finally she moved both legs slightly under the sheet. I'm not paralyzed, she realized with joy. Then a terrible stab of pain ran through her left leg and she felt herself start to black out again. She fought to stay awake.

Dr. Demuth was saying, "Poor kid. The way that ligament's torn I doubt she'll ever dance again."

Not dance again! A scream welled up from deep down inside Leah. She tried to open her mouth to say, "I'll dance again. *I will,*" but she never got the words out. She was too tired even to speak.

From very far away Leah seemed to hear Madame. "Medicine may be your field, young man, but I know my dancers. And I promise you that Leah Stephenson *will* dance again. . . . It'll take all your medicine, plus a lot of hard work, patience, and lots of rest and recuperation." Madame kept talking, but her voice grew very dim, as if she was leaving the room. Leah wanted to call her back, but she couldn't. She felt as if her lips had been glued together.

The doctor had said that he doubted Leah would ever dance again, but Madame had promised that she would—and Madame never made a promise she couldn't keep. As Leah drifted into a deep sleep, the question kept running through her mind, over and over, until she thought she would go crazy: *Will I dance again?*

GLOSSARY

Adagio Slow tempo dance steps; essential to sustaining controlled body line. When dancing with a partner, the term refers to support of ballerina.

Allegro Quick, lively dance step.

Arabesque Dancer stands on one leg and extends the other leg straight back while holding the arms in graceful positions.

Arabesque penchée The dancer's whole body leans forward over the supporting leg. (Also referred to as penché.)

Assemblé A jump in which the two feet are brought together in the air before the dancer lands on the ground in fifth position.

Attitude turns The *attitude* is a classical position in which the working or raised leg is bent at the knee and extended to the back, as if wrapped around the dancer. An *attitude turn* is a turn performed in this position.

Ballon Illusion of suspending in air.

Barre The wooden bar along the wall of every ballet studio. Work at the barre makes up the first part of practice.

Battement Throwing the leg as high as possible into the air to the front, the side, and the back. Several variations.

  Battement en cloche Swinging the leg as high as possible to the back and to the front to loosen the hip joint.

Batterie A series of movements in which the feet are beaten together.

  Grande batterie Refers to steps with high elevation.

  Petite batterie Steps with small elevation.

Bourrée Small, quick steps usually done on toes. Many variations.

Brisé A jump off one foot in which the legs are beaten together in the air.

Cabriole A step in which the dancer extends one leg to the front, back or side, and, springing upwards, brings the second leg up to the first before landing.

Centre work The main part of practice; performing steps on the floor after barre work.

Chainé A series of short, usually fast turns on pointe by which a dancer moves across the stage.

Corps de ballet Any and all members of the ballet who are not soloists.

Dégagé Extension with toe pointed in preparation for a ballet step.

Developpé The slow raising and unfolding of one leg until it is high in the air (usually done in pas de deux, or with support of barre or partner).

Divertissement A series of entertaining and/or technically brilliant dances performed within a ballet. For example, as in the Marzipan dance of *The Nutcracker* or in the Bluebird Variation in the last act of *Sleeping Beauty*.

Echappé A movement in which the dancer springs up from fifth position onto pointe in second position. Also a jump.

Enchaînement A sequence of two or more steps.

Entrechat A spring into the air from the fifth position in which the extended legs (with feet well pointed) criss-cross at the lower calf.

Fouetté A step in which the dancer is on one leg and uses the other leg in a sort of whipping movement to help the body turn.

Frappé (or *battement frappé*) A barre exercise in which the dancer extends the foot of the working leg to the front, side and back, striking the ball of the foot on the ground. Dancer then stretches the toe until it is slightly off the ground and returns the foot *sure le cou-de-pieds* (on the ankle) against the ankle of the supporting leg.

Glissade A gliding step across the floor.

Jeté A jump from one foot onto the other in which working leg appears to be thrown in the air.

   Jeté en tournant A jeté performed while turning.

Mazurka A Polish national dance.

Pas de deux Dance for 2 dancers. ("Pas de trois" means dance for 3 dancers, and so on.)

Pas de chat Meaning "step of the cat". A light, springing movement. The dancer jumps and draws one foot up to the knee of the opposite leg, then draws up the other leg, one after the other, traveling diagonally across the stage.

Penché Referring to an arabesque penchée.

Piqué Direct step onto pointe without bending the knee of the working leg.

Plié With feet and legs turned out, a movement by which the dancer bends both knees outward over her toes, leaving her heels on the ground.

   Demi plié Bending the knees as far as possible leaving the heels on the floor.

   Grand plié Bending knees all the way down, letting the heels come off the floor (except in second position).

Pointe work Exercises performed in pointe (toe) shoes.

Port de bras Position of the dancer's arms.

Posé Stepping onto pointe with a straight leg.

Positions There are five basic positions of the feet and arms that all ballet dancers must learn.

Rétiré Drawing the toe of one foot to the opposite knee.

Rond de jambe à terre An exercise performed at the barre to loosen the hip joint: performed first outward (*en dehors*) and then inward (*en dedans*). The working leg is extended first to the front with the foot fully pointed and then swept around to the side and back and through first position to the front again. The movement is then reversed, starting from the fourth positon back and sweeping around to the side and front. (The foot traces the shape of the letter "D" on the floor.)

Sissonne With a slight plié, dancer springs into the air from the fifth position, and lands on one foot with a demi plié with the other leg extended to the back, front, or side. The foot of the extended leg is then closed to the supporting foot.

Tendu Stretching or holding a certain position or movement.

Tour en l'air A spectacular jump in which the dancer leaps directly upwards and turns one, two or three times before landing.

Here's a look at what's ahead in STARTING OVER, the eleventh book in Fawcett's "Satin Slippers" series for GIRLS ONLY

"Go on, Leah!" Chrissy nudged her in the back.

Leah nodded. There was no turning back. Dancing was her dream, and if starting over meant starting out in front of these kids who seemed to know everything about her and who probably expected her to be good, then that's what she had to do. Living up to her reputation wasn't important right now—dancing again was. Leah took a deep breath and quietly walked to the very back of the room. She sat down, with Chrissy just a yard or so away, and tried to concentrate on her warm-ups. But she could feel ten pairs of children's eyes upon her. Over the past couple of months she had completely forgotten that she was famous.

Infamous is more like it, Leah was thinking a few minutes later at the barre. She hadn't even gotten through her second set of grand pliés in first position. Her knees felt like jelly, her thighs were trembling, and her ankles felt as stiff as steel. Her left one felt as though it were held together by tightly wound springs.

"Don't force yourself, Leah." Miss Greene walked up behind her and in a quiet voice continued, "This is your first class back. I don't want you to do more than the tendus, and maybe you should stop before that.

Stop while you're ahead!" she warned, and continued to stroll around the room, correcting the children one by one.

"Maybe I *should* just stop!" Leah cried as the music changed and the girls shifted to fifth position. Leah attempted the first plié, but her legs, her foot, and her back told her it was impossible. She took her hand off the barre and faced Miss Greene.

"Leah, I know it's hard, but—"

Leah didn't give her former teacher time to finish. Covering her face with her hands, she ran out of the room. She stumbled into the changing room, her ankle suddenly throbbing and her knees weak. She sank down in front of the long wooden bench and buried her face in her arms. Her slender body was racked with sobs. What had possessed her, today of all days, to try to dance again?

"Leah?" Chrissy sat down beside Leah and smoothed her back with her hand. "Gee, you didn't look that bad!" she said.

"Look bad!" Leah gulped back her tears and a kind of strangled laugh forced its way up her throat. "Chrissy, I don't care how I look, I care how I feel. And that's awful!"

She stretched her legs out in front of her and kneaded her muscles with her hands. "I can't do it, Chrissy. My legs hurt so much. And my ankle and foot!" She tried to circle her ankle around, without success.

"It's your first class back," Chrissy pointed out. "What do you expect?"

Leah looked up at Chrissy and bluntly asked, "What do you know about it? You're not a dancer!"

Chrissy looked injured. "I'm just trying to help," she mumbled. She began stripping off her own dance gear. "If you want to give up so easily, it's none of my business, is it!" she said, a hint of anger in her big brown eyes.

Before Leah could reply, Miss Greene walked into the changing room. Both girls scrambled to their feet, but Leah gasped as she put weight on her left foot and sank back down on the bench.

"Deborah is taking the class for the moment," Miss Greene explained. She sat down next to Leah. "Now, what are all these dramatics about, Stephenson?"

The familiar, slightly scornful tone of her old teacher's voice had an oddly calming effect on Leah. She gulped back her tears and rubbed her arm across her face.

Spotting Leah's bare back and shoulders, Miss Greene grabbed a shawl from a rack of costumes and tossed it to her. "No point adding cramped muscles to all your other problems now. And get some leg warmers on quick, or get dressed!" she commanded.

Leah reached for her jeans. She kicked off her slippers, but still didn't know what to say to Miss Greene.

"So, you're going to give up that easily!" the dark-haired woman said caustically.

Leah's head snapped up. "Why not? I mean, it's obvious, isn't it?" She stuck out her left leg. "It doesn't work anymore. I can't even do a children's beginner-class barre!"

"No, you can't," Miss Greene agreed.

Leah's heart sank a little. She had somehow expected Miss Greene to contradict her, to say she was wrong.

"In fact, you will probably not be able to get through any kind of barre for about a week or so, even if you come to class every day. Even then you'll feel crummy by the end of the barre," Miss Greene continued.

"But she *will* be able to dance again, won't she?" Chrissy asked.

Miss Greene looked from Chrissy to Leah and shrugged. "That's up to her, isn't it?"

"I tried just now, I really tried!" Leah defended herself.

"Yes, you did. And you probably did exactly the right amount of work for today. And I know from experience," Miss Greene added pointedly, "exactly how awful you felt out there. But Leah, you have to face facts. You've been seriously hurt, and now it's time to begin again."

"Begin again!" Leah repeated faintly. "I can't begin all over again, not now. I'm already sixteen. I'll be too old."

"Beginning again at sixteen after all your training is not like starting from scratch, Leah. But you will have to go slowly, and carefully. But I guarantee you—if you really *want* to dance as much as you've said you do—then you will someday again," Miss Greene said.

ABOUT THE AUTHOR

ELIZABETH BERNARD has had a lifelong passion for dance. Her interest and background in ballet is wide and various and has led to many friendships and acquaintances in the ballet and dance world. Through these connections she has had the opportunity to witness firsthand a behind-the-scenes world of dance seldom seen by non-dancers. She is familiar with the stuff of ballet life: the artistry, the dedication, the fierce competition, the heartaches, the pains, and disappointments. She is the author of over two dozen books for young adults, including titles in the bestselling COUPLES series, published by Scholastic, and the SISTERS series, published by Fawcett.